Chinese Mythology
Gods, Goddesses, Monkeys, Eternal Beings, and More

By Sally Stephens

If you like my book, please leave a review. I would appreciate it. Thank you!

Table of Contents

Chapter 1: The Sociology of the Chinese

In spite of much research and conjecture, the beginning of the Chinese people remains undetermined. We do not know who they were nor whence they came. Such proof as there is points to their immigration from elsewhere; the Chinese themselves have a tradition of a Western beginning. The first picture we have of their actual history shows us, not a people acting just as if long settled in a land which was their home and that of their predecessors, but an alien race combating with wild beasts, clearing dense forests, and driving back the aboriginal occupants.

Setting aside several theories (including the one that the Chinese are autochthonous and their society indigenous) now concerned by the best authorities as untenable, the looks into of sinologists seem to show an origin (1) in early Akkadia; or (2) in Khotan, the Tarim valley (normally what is now referred to as Eastern Turkestan), or the K'un- lun Mountains (concerning which more presently). The 2nd hypothesis may relate only to a layover of longer or much shorter period en route from Akkadia to the supreme settlement in China, particularly since the Khotan society has been revealed to have been imported from the Punjab in the 3rd century B.C. The fact that some bad mistakes have been made relating to the recognitions of early Chinese rulers with Babylonian kings, and of the Chinese po-hsing (Cantonese bak-sing) 'people' with the Bak Sing or Bak tribes, doesn't exclude the possibility of an Akkadian origin. But in either case the immigration into China was most likely gradual, and may have taken the route from Western or Main Asia direct to the banks of the Yellow River, or may potentially have followed that to the south-east through Burma and then to the north-east through what is now China-- the settlement of the latter country having actually thus spread from south-west to north-east, or in a north-easterly direction along the Yangtzŭ River, and so north, instead of, as is normally supposed, from north to south.

Southern Origin Improbable
However this latter path would present tons of difficulties; it would seem to have been put forward simply as ancillary to the theory that the Chinese come from the Indo-Chinese peninsula. This theory is based upon the presumptions that the ancient Chinese ideograms include representations of tropical animals and plants; that the oldest and purest forms of the language are found in the south; and that the Chinese and the Indo-Chinese groups of languages are both tonal. However all of these truths or supposed facts are as quickly or better represented by the supposition that the Chinese shown up from the north or north-west in succeeding waves of migration, the later arrivals pushing the earlier further and further toward the south, so that the oldest and purest types of Chinese would be found just where they are, the tonal languages of the Indo-Chinese peninsula remaining in that case regarded as the languages of the vanguard of the migration. Also, the ideograms referred to represent animals and plants of the temperate zone instead of the tropics, but even if it could be revealed, which it cannot, that these animals and plants now belong specifically to the tropics, that would be no

evidence of the tropical beginning of the Chinese, for in the earliest times the environment of North China was much milder than it is now, and animals like tigers and elephants existed in the thick jungles which are later found only in more southern latitudes.

Growth of Races from North to South

The theory of a southern origin (to which an additional serious objection will be stated currently) implies a steady seepage of Chinese immigrants through South or Mid-China (as above suggested) toward the north, but there is little doubt that the movement of the races has been from north to south and not vice versa. In what are now the provinces of Western Kansu and Ssŭch' uan there lived a people associated to the Chinese (as proved by the research study of Indo-Chinese comparative philology) who moved into the present area of Tibet and are known as Tibetans; in what is now the province of Yünnan were the Shan or Ai-lao (modern Laos), who, forced by Mongol intrusions, emigrated to the peninsula in the south and became the Siamese; and in Indo-China, unrelated to the Chinese, were the Annamese, Khmer, Mon, Khasi, Colarains (whose residues are dispersed over the hill tracts of Central India), and other people, extending in prehistoric times into Southern China, but consequently driven back by the growth of the Chinese in that direction.

Arrival of the Chinese in China

Taking into account all the existing proof, the objections to all other theories of the origin of the Chinese appear to be greater than any yet raised to the theory that immigrants from the Tarim valley or beyond (i.e. from Elam or Akkadia, either direct or via Eastern Turkestan) struck the banks of the Yellow River in their eastward journey and followed its course till they reached the localities where we first find them settled, namely, in the region covered by parts of the three modern-day provinces of Shansi, Shensi, and Honan where their frontiers join. They were then (about 2500 or 3000 B.C.) in a reasonably sophisticated state of civilization. The nation east and south of the district was occupied by aboriginal people, with whom the Chinese fought, as they did with the wild animals and the dense vegetation, but with whom they also commingled and intermarried, and among whom they planted groups as centres from which to spread their culture.

The K'un- lun Mountains

With with reference to the K'un- lun Mountains, designated in Chinese mythology as the abode of the gods-- the ancestors of the Chinese race-- it needs to be kept in mind that these are determined not with the range dividing Tibet from Chinese Turkestan, but with the Hindu Kush. That brings us somewhat nearer to Babylon, and the obvious merging of the 2 theories, the Central Asian and the Western Asian, would appear to point to a possible resolution of the problem. Nü Kua, among the alleged creators of human beings, and Nü and Kua, the very first two human entities (according to a variation of the legend), are put in the K'un- lun Mountains. That looks hopeful. Unfortunately, the K'un- lun legend is shown to be of Taoist beginning. K'un- lun is the main mountain of the world, and 3000 miles in height. There is the fountain of immortality, and thence flow the four great rivers of the world. In other words, it is the Sumêru of Hindu folklore transplanted into Chinese legend, and for our present purpose without historic value.

It would take up way too much space to explain of this fascinating problem of the origin of the Chinese and their society, the cultural connexions or similarities of China and Western Asia in pre-Babylonian times, the origin of the two distinct culture-areas so marked throughout the greater part of Chinese history, etc., and it will be sufficient for our present purpose to mention the conclusion to which the evidence points.

Provisionary Conclusion
Pending the discovery of definitive evidence, the following provisional conclusion has much to advise it-- particularly, that the ancestors of the Chinese people came from the west, from Akkadia or Elam, or from Khotan, or (more most likely) from Akkadia or Elam via Khotan, as one wanderer or pastoral tribe or group of nomad or pastoral tribes, or as succeeding waves of immigrants, reached what is now China Appropriate at its north-west corner, settled round the elbow of the Yellow River, spread north-eastward, eastward, and southward, conquering, absorbing, or pushing right before them the aborigines into what is now South and South-west China. These aboriginal races, who represent a wave or waves of neolithic immigrants from Western Asia earlier than the relatively high-headed immigrants into North China (who came about the twenty-fifth or twenty-fourth century B.C.), and who have left so deep an impress on the Japanese, mixed and intermarried with the Chinese in the south, eventually producing the noticable differences, in physical, mental, and psychological qualities, in beliefs, ideas, languages, procedures, and products, from the Northern Chinese which are so obvious at the present day.

Chapter 2: Inorganic Environment

At the beginning of their recognized history the nation occupied by the Chinese was the comparatively little area above pointed out. It was then a tract of an irregular elongate shape, lying between latitude 34 ° and 40 ° N. and longitude 107 ° and 114 ° E. This area round the elbow of the Yellow River had a part of about 50,000 square miles, and was gradually extended to the sea-coast on the north-east as far as longitude 119 °, when its location was about doubled. It had a population of maybe a million, increasing with the growth to 2 million. This may be called infant China. Its duration (the Feudal Duration) was in the 2 thousand years between the twenty-fourth and third centuries B.C. During the first centuries of the Monarchical Duration, which lasted from 221 B.C. to A.D. 1912, it had expanded to the south to such an extent that it included all of the Eighteen Provinces constituting what is called China Proper of modern times, with the exception of a part of the west of Kansu and the greater parts of Ssŭch'uan and Yünnan. At the time of the Manchu conquest at the beginning of the seventeenth century A.D. it embraced all the territory lying between latitude 18 ° and 40 ° N. and longitude 98 ° and 122 ° E. (the Eighteen Provinces or China Correct), with the addition of the huge distant territories of Manchuria, Mongolia, Ili, Koko-nor, Tibet, and Corea, with suzerainty over Burma and Annam-- an area of more than 5,000,000 square miles, consisting of the 2,000,000 square miles covered by the Eighteen Provinces. Usually, this area is mountainous in the west, sloping gradually down toward the sea on the east. It contains 3 chief series of mountains and large alluvial plains in the north, east, and south. 3 great and about thirty large rivers intersect the nation, their numerous tributaries reaching every part of it.

As concerns geological features, the great alluvial plains rest upon granite, brand-new red sandstone, or limestone. In the north is found the peculiar loess formation, having its origin probably in the built up dust of ages blown from the Mongolian plateau. The passage from north to south is generally from the older to the more recent rocks; from east to west a comparable series is found, with some volcanic features in the west and south. Coal and iron are the chief minerals, gold, silver, copper, lead, tin, jade, and so on, being also mined.

The climate of the vast location is not consistent. In the north the winter season is long and rigorous, the summertime hot and dry, with a short rainy season in July and August; in the south the summer season is long, hot, and wet, the winter short. The mean temperature level is 50.3 ° F. and 70 ° F. in the north and south respectively. Typically, the thermometer is low for the latitude, though maybe it is more correct to say that the Gulf Stream raises the temperature level of the west coast of Europe above the average. The mean rainfall in the north is 16, in the south 70 inches, with variations in other parts. Tropical storms blow in the south between July and October.

The wild animals consist of the tiger, panther, leopard, bear, sable, otter, monkey, wolf, fox, twenty-seven or more species of ruminants, and many species of rodents. The rhinoceros, elephant, and tapir still exist in Yünnan. The domestic animals consist of the camel and the water-buffalo. There are about 700 species of birds, and innumerable species of fishes and insects.

Chapter 3: Sociological Environment

On their arrival in what is now called China the Chinese, as already noted, battled with the aboriginal tribes. The latter were gotten rid of, taken in, or driven south with the spread of Chinese rule. The Chinese "chosen the eyes of the land," and consequently the non-Chinese people now live in the unhealthy forests or marshes of the south, or in mountain areas tough of access, some even in trees (a voluntary, not compulsory big promotion), though several, just like the Dog Jung in Fukien, keep settlements like isles amongst the ruling race.

In the 3rd century B.C. started the hostile relations of the Chinese with the northern nomads, which continued throughout the majority of their history. During the very first six centuries A.D. there was intercourse with Rome, Parthia, Turkey, Mesopotamia, Ceylon, India, and Indochina, and in the seventh century with the Arabs. Europe was brought within the sociological environment by Christian tourists. From the tenth to the 13th century the north was occupied by Kitans and Nüchêns, and the entire Empire was under Mongol sway for eighty-eight years in the 13th and fourteenth centuries. Relations of a commercial and spiritual nature were held with neighbours during the following 4 hundred years. Routine diplomatic sexual intercourse with Western countries was developed as a result of a series of wars in the eighteenth and nineteenth centuries. Till recently the country held aloof from alliances and was typically averse to foreign sexual intercourse. From 1537 onward, as a follow up of war or treaty, concessions, settlements, and so on, were gotten by foreign Powers. China has now lost some of her border countries and large adjacent islands, the army and business pressure of Western nations and Japan having actually taken the place of the military pressure of the Tartars already referred to. The great issue for her, a farming nation, is how to find methods and the military spirit to preserve her integrity, the further violation of which could not but be concerned by the student of sociological history as a great tragedy and a world-wide catastrophe.

Physical, Psychological, and Intellectual Characters
The physical characters of the Chinese are too well known to need comprehensive recital. The original immigrants into North China all came from blond races, but the modern Chinese have little left of the immigrant stock. The oblique, almond-shaped eyes, with black iris and the orbits far apart, have a vertical fold of skin over the inner canthus, concealing a part of the iris, a peculiarity identifying the eastern races of Asia from all other families of man. The stature and weight of brain are generally beneath the average. The hair is black, coarse, and round; the beard scanty or missing. The colour of the skin is darker in the south than in the north.

Mentally the Chinese are sober, industrious, of remarkable endurance, grateful, considerate, and ceremonious, with a high sense of mercantile honour, but timorous, vicious, unsympathetic, mendacious, and libidinous.

Intellectually they were till recently, and to a large degree still are, non-progressive, in chains to harmony and system in culture, imitative, unimaginative, torpid, indirect, suspicious, and superstitious.

The character is being customized by intercourse with other tribes of the earth and by the strong force of physical, intellectual, and moral education.

Marital Relationship in Early Times

Certain parts of the marital relationship ceremonial of China as now existing suggest that the original form of marital relationship was by capture-- of which, certainly, there is proof in the classical Book of Odes. But a routine form of marital relationship (in reality an agreement of sale) is revealed to have existed in the earliest historical times. The form was not monogamous, though it appears soon to have assumed that of a qualified monogamy including one spouse and one or more courtesans, the number of the latter being as a rule restricted only by the methods of the husband. The higher the rank the larger was the number of courtesans and handmaids in addition to the marriage partner proper, the palaces of the kings and princes including some hundreds of them. This form it has kept to the present day, though associations now exist for the abolition of concubinage. In early times, along with throughout the whole of Chinese history, concubinage was in fact universal, and there is some evidence also of polyandry (which, however, cannot have prevailed to any great level). The age for marriage was twenty for the man and fifteen for the girl, celibacy after thirty and twenty respectively being formally discouraged. In the province of Shantung it was usual for the wives to be older than their husbands. The mother's and father's consent to the betrothal was sought through the intervention of a matchmaker, the proposal coming from with the parents, and the wishes of the future bride and bridegroom not being considered. The conclusion of the marital relationship was the progress of the bride-to-be from the home of her parents to that of the bridegroom, where after numerous events she and he worshipped his ancestors together, the praise amounting to little bit more than a statement of the union to the ancestral spirits. After a short layover with her spouse the bride-to-be revisited her father and mother, and the marriage was not considered as finally consummated till after this visit had taken place.

The status of women was low, and the power of the spouse great-- so great that he could kill his wife with impunity. Divorce was common, and all in favour of the husband, who, while he could not be separated by her, could put his spouse away for disobedience or perhaps for loquaciousness. A widower remarried immediately, but rejection to remarry by a widow was esteemed an act of chastity. She often mutilated herself or perhaps committed suicide to stop remarriage, and was posthumously honoured for doing so. Being her partner's as much in the Otherworld as in this, remarriage would engage of the character of unchastity and insubordination; the argument, obviously, not using to the case of the spouse, who by remarriage simply adds another member to his clan without infringing on anybody's rights.

Marriage in Monarchical and Republican Periods

The marital system of the early classical times, of which the above were the basics, changed but little bit throughout the long period of monarchical rule lasting from 221 B.C. to A.D. 1912. The principal item, as before, was to protect a successor to sacrifice to the spirits of departed progenitors. Marriage was elective, but old bachelors and old maids were really limited. The courtesans went through the spouse, who was thought about to be the mother of their children in addition to her own. Her status, though, was not considerably superior. Implicit obedience was exacted from her. She could not have property, but could not be hired for prostitution. The latter vice was common, in spite of the early age at which marriage took place and in spite of the system of concubinage-- which is after all but a legalized transfer of prostitutional cohabitation to the domestic circle.

Since the facility of the Republic in 1912 the 'landslide' in the direction of Western progress has had its influence also on the domestic organizations. However while the essentials of the marriage agreement stay virtually the same as before, the most conspicuous changes have been in the accompanying ceremonial-- now in some cases rather foreign, but in a large, maybe the best, number of cases that repellent thing, half foreign, half Chinese; as, for instance, when the procession, otherwise native, includes foreign glass-panelled carriages, or the bridegroom wears a 'bowler' or top-hat with his Chinese dress-- and in the greater freedom permitted to women, who are seen out of doors far more than previously, sit at table with their spouses, attend public functions and suppers, gown mainly in foreign fashion, and play tennis and other games, instead of being detainees of the 'inner apartment or condo' and home drudges bit better than servants.

One unforeseen result of the increased flexibility is definitely impressive, and is one not very likely to have been predicted by the most far-sighted sociologist. A lot of the 'progressive' Chinese, now that it is the fashion for Chinese wives to be seen in public with their spouses, finding the ignorant, gauche, small-footed household drudge unable to take on the smarter foreign-educated wives of their neighbours, have actually repudiated them and taken unto themselves spouses whom they can show in public without 'loss of face'! It is, though, only fair to add that the overall number of these cases, however by no methods inconsiderable, appears to be proportionately small.

Parents and Children
As was the power of the partner over the marriage partner, so was that of the father over his kids. Infanticide (due chiefly to hardship, and varying with it) was frequent, specifically in the case of female children, who were but a little esteemed; the practice dominating extensively in 3 or four provinces, less thoroughly in other ones, and being virtually absent in a large number. Beyond the simple fact that some charges were enacted against it by the Emperor Ch' ien Lung (A.D. 1736-- 96), and that by statute it was a capital offence to murder kids in order to use parts of their bodies for medicine, it was not legally restricted. When the abuse ended up being too scandalous in any district pronouncements condemning it would be released by the local authorities. A man might, by purchase and agreement, adopt an individual as son, daughter, or grandchild, such person acquiring therefore all the rights of a daughter or son. Descent, both of real and personal property, was to all the sons of partners and courtesans as joint heirs, regardless of seniority. Bastards received half shares. Estates were not divisible by the kids throughout the lifetime of their mom and dad or grandparents.

The head of the family being but the life-renter of the family property, bound by set rules, wills were superfluous, and were used only where the customary respect for the parents gave them a voice in arranging the specifics of the succession. For this purpose spoken or written guidelines were typically given.

In the absence of the father, the male relatives of the same surname assumed the protectorship of the young. The protector exercised full authority and took pleasure in the surplus revenues of his ward's estate, but may not alienate the property.

There are many instances in Chinese history of severe devotion of kids to parents taking the form of self-wounding and even of suicide in the hope of curing father's and mother's diseases or saving their lives.

Political History
The country populated by the Chinese on their arrival from the West was, as we saw, the district where the modern-day provinces of Shansi, Shensi, and Honan join. This they extended in an easterly direction to the coasts of the Gulf of Chihli-- a stretch of area about 600 miles long by 300 broad. The population, as already specified, was between one and 2 millions. During the very first two 1,000 years of their recognized history the boundaries of this area were not significantly bigger, but beyond the more or less undefined borderland to the south were chou or people, nuclei of Chinese population, which continually increased in size through conquest of the neighbouring territory. In 221 B.C. all the feudal states into which this territory had been shelled out, and which combated with one another, were subjugated and absorbed by the state of Ch'in, which in that year set up the monarchical form of federal government-- the form which obtained in China for the next twenty-one centuries.

Though the origin of the name 'China' has not yet been finally determined, the best authorities regard it as stemmed from the name of the feudal state of Ch'in.

Under this short-lived dynasty of Ch'in and the famous Han dynasty (221 B.C. to A.D. 221) which followed it, the Empire broadened until it embraced nearly all the territory now known as China Proper (the Eighteen Provinces of Manchu times). To these were added in order between 194 B.C. and A.D. 1414: Corea, Sinkiang (the New Area or Eastern Turkestan), Manchuria, Formosa, Tibet, and Mongolia-- Formosa and Corea being annexed by Japan in 1895 and 1910 respectively. Numerous other extra-China nations and islands, gotten and lost throughout the long course of Chinese history (at one time, from 73 to 48 B.C., "all Asia from Japan to the Caspian Sea was tributary to the Middle Kingdom," i.e. China), it is not necessary to point out here. Throughout the Southern Sung dynasty (1127-- 1280) the Tartars owned the northern half of China, as far down as the Yangtzŭ River, and in the Yüan dynasty (1280-- 1368) they dominated the entire country. During the duration 1644-- 1912 it was in the belongings of the Manchus. At present the five chief component tribes of China are represented in the striped nationwide flag (from the leading downward) by red (Manchus), yellow (Chinese), blue (Mongolians), white (Mohammedans), and black (Tibetans). This flag was adopted on the establishment of the Republic in 1912, and supplanted the triangular Dragon flag previously in use. By this time the population-- which had varied considerably at different periods owing to war, scarcity, and plague-- had increased to about 400,000,000.

Chapter 4: The Government

The general department of the nation was into the King and the People, The former was considered as selected by the will of Heaven and as the moms and dad of the latter. Besides being king, he was also law-giver, commander-in-chief of the armies, high priest, and master of ceremonies. The people were separated into four classes: (1) Shih, Officers (later Scholars), including Ch' ên, Authorities (a few of whom were ennobled), and Shên Shih, Gentry; (2) Nung, Agriculturists; (3) Kung, Artisans; and (4) Shang, Merchants.

For administrative purposes there were at the seat of central government (which, initially at P'ing- yang-- in modern Shansi-- was moved eleven times throughout the Feudal Period, and was finally at Yin) ministers, or ministers and a hierarchy of officials, the country being split into provinces, varying in number from nine in the earliest times to thirty-six under the First Emperor, 221 B.C., and finally twenty-two at the present day. In the beginning these provinces included states, which were models of the central state, the ruler's 'Middle Kingdom.' The provincial administration was in the hands of twelve Pastors or Lord-Lieutenants. They were the chiefs of all the nobles in a province. Civil and army offices were not separated. The feudal lords or princes of states typically lived at the king's court, officers of that court being also sent forth as princes of states. The king was the source of legislation and administered justice. The princes in their several states had the power of rewards and punishments. Profits was stemmed from a tithe on the land, from the income of artisans, merchants, anglers, foresters, and from the homage brought by savage tribes.

The general structure and concepts of the system of administration stayed the same, with few variations, down to the end of the Monarchical Period in 1912. At the end of that period we find the emperor still thought about as of divine descent, still the head of the civil, legislative, army, ecclesiastical, and ritualistic administration, with the nation still divided into the same 4 classes. The chief ministries at the capital, Peking, could most of the times trace their descent from their models of feudal times, and the primary provincial administrative officials-- the Governor-General or Viceroy, governor, provincial treasurer, judge, etc.-- had similarly a pedigree running back to offices then existing-- a continuous duration of adherence to type which is most likely distinct.

Appointment to office was at initially by selection, followed by an evaluation to check efficiency; later was introduced the system of public competitive literary assessments for office, fully organized in the seventeenth century, and eliminated in 1903, when official positions were tossed open to the graduates of colleges established on a contemporary basis.

In 1912, on the defeat of the Manchu monarchy, China became a republic, with an elected President, and a Parliament consisting of a Senate and House of Representatives. The numerous government departments were rearranged on Western lines, and a ton of new workplaces instituted. Approximately the present year the Law of the Constitution, owing to political dissension between the North and the South, has not been put into force.

Laws

Chinese law, like primitive law usually, was not set up so as to make sure justice between man and man; its item was to impose subordination of the ruled to the ruler. The laws were punitive and vindictive rather than reformatory or restorative, criminal rather than civil. Penalties were harsh: branding, cutting off the nose, the legs at the knees, castration, and death, the latter not necessarily, or certainly ordinarily, for taking life. They included in some cases penalty of the family, the clan, and the neighbours of the offender. The lex talionis was in full blast.

However, in spite of the extreme nature of the punishments, possibly adapted, more or less, to a harsh state of society, though the "appropriate end of punishments"-- to "make an end of penalizing"-- was really missed, the Chinese developed a series of exceptional legal codes. This series began with the revision of King Mu's Punishments in 950 B.C., the first routine code being issued in 650 B.C., and ended with the popular Ta Ch'ing lü li (Laws and Statutes of the Great Ch'ing Dynasty), provided in A.D. 1647. Of these codes the great prototype was the Law Traditional prepared by Li K'uei (Li K'uei fa ching), a statesman in the service of the first ruler of the Wei State, in the 4th century B.C. The Ta Ch'ing lü li has been highly praised by proficient judges. Originally it approved only 2 types of penalty, death and flogging, but others were in use, and the barbarous ling ch'ih, 'lingering death' or 'slicing to pieces,' developed about A.D. 1000 and abolished in 1905, was inflicted for high treason, parricide, on women who killed their husbands, and murderers of 3 individuals of one family. In fact, until some first-hand knowledge of Western systems and process was obtained, the vindictive as opposed to the reformatory idea of penalties continued to get in China down to rather recent years, and has not yet totally vanished. Though the crueller kinds of punishment had been legally abolished, they continued to be used in tons of parts. Having actually been joint judge at Chinese trials at which, in spite of my protests, detainees were hung up by their thumbs and made to kneel on chains to extort confession (without which no implicated person could be penalized), I can testify that the real meaning of the "proper end of punishments" ran out participated in the Chinese mind at the close of the monarchical régime than it had 4000 years in the past.

As a result of the reform movement into which China was pushed as an alternative to foreign domination towards the end of the Manchu Period, but mainly owing to the bait held out by Western Powers, that extraterritoriality would be eliminated when China had reformed her judicial system, a brand-new Provisional Criminal Code was published. It replaced death by hanging or strangulation for decapitation, and jail time for various lengths of time for bambooing. It was adopted in large procedure by the Republican régime and is the primary legal instrument in usage at the present time. But close evaluation reveals the fact that it is almost a precise copy of the Japanese penal code, which in turn was modelled upon that of Germany. It is, in fact, a Western code imitated, and as it stands is rather out of harmony with present conditions in China. It will have to be customized and modified to be an ideal, just, and practicable nationwide legal instrument for the Chinese people. Additionally, it is often overridden in a high-handed way by the authorities, who often keep a person acquitted by the

Courts of Justice in custody till they have 'squeezed' him of all they can hope to get out of him. And it is notable that, though arrangement was made in the Draft Code for trial by jury, this arrangement never entered into influence; and the slavish replica of alien approaches is revealed by the strangely enough irregular reason given-- that "the fact that jury trials have been eliminated in Japan is a sign of the inadvisability of transplanting this Western institution into China!"

City government
The central administration being a remote network of officialdom, there was hardly any room for local government apart from it. We find it only in the village elder and those related to him, who took up what federal government was necessary where the jurisdiction of the system of the central administration-- the district magistracy-- stopped, or at least did not issue itself in meddling much.

Chapter 5: Institutions in Society

Armed force System

The peace-loving farming settlers in early China had at first no army. When occasion emerged, all the armers exchanged their ploughshares for swords and bows and arrows and went forth to combat. In the periods between the harvests, when the fields were clear, they held manoeuvres and practised the arts of warfare. The king, who had his Six Armies, under the 6 High Nobles, forming the royal army force, led the troops face to face, accompanied by the spirit-tablets of his forefathers and of the gods of the land and grain. Chariots, drawn by 4 horses and consisting of soldiers armed with spears and javelins and archers, were much in usage. A 1,000 chariots were the regular force. Warriors wore buskins on their legs and were often gagged in order to stop the alarm being provided to the enemy. In action the chariots occupied the center, the bowmen the left, the spearmen the right flank. Elephants were in some cases used in attack. Spy-kites, signal-flags, hook-ladders, horns, cymbals, drums, and beacon-fires were in usage. The ears of the vanquished were brought to the king, quarter being rarely if ever given.

After the establishment of absolute monarchical government standing armies ended up being the rule. Military science was taught, and soldiers often trained for seven years. Chariots with upper floors or spy-towers were used for battling in narrow defiles, and hollow squares were formed of combined chariots, infantry, and dragoons. The weakness of disunion of forces was well understood. In the 6th century A.D. the massed soldiers numbered about a million and a quarter. In A.D. 627 there was an efficient standing army of 900,000 men, the term of service being from the ages of twenty to sixty. Throughout the Mongol dynasty (1280-- 1368) there was a navy of 5000 ships manned by 70,000 trained fighters. The Mongols totally revolutionized methods and enhanced on all the army knowledge of the time. In 1614 the Manchu 'Eight Banners,' composed of Manchus, Mongolians, and Chinese, were instituted. The provincial forces, designated the Army of the Green Standard, were divided into land forces and marine forces, superseded on active duty by 'braves' (yung), or irregulars, enlisted and discharged according to scenarios. After the war with Japan in 1894 reforms were seriously undertaken, with the result that the army has now been modernized in gown, weapons, techniques, etc., and is by no means a negligible quantity on the planet's battling forces. A modern navy is also being obtained by structure and purchase. For a lot of centuries the soldier, being, like the priest, ineffective, was related to with disdain, and now that his indispensableness for defensive purposes is recognized he needs to fight not only any actual opponent who might attack him, but those far subtler forces from over the sea which seem likely to acquire supremacy in his army councils, if not actual control of his whole army system. It is, in my view, the duty of Western countries to take steps before it is too late to prevent this great disaster.

Ecclesiastical Institutions

The dancing and chanting exorcists called wu were the first Chinese priests, with temples consisting of gods worshipped and sacrificed to, but there was no special sacerdotal class. Worship of Paradise could only be performed by the king or emperor. Ecclesiastical and political functions were not entirely separated. The king was pontifex maximus, the nobles, statesmen, and civil and military officers served as priests, the ranks being similar to those of the political hierarchy. Praise took place in the 'Hall of Light,' which was also a palace and audience and council chamber. Sacrifices were offered to Heaven, the hills and rivers, forefathers, and all the spirits. Dancing held a conspicuous spot in worship. Idols are spoken of in the earliest times.

Of course, each faith, as it formed itself out of the original ancestor-worship, had its own spiritual places, functionaries, observances, ritualistic. Hence, at the State praise of Paradise, Nature, and so on, there were the 'Great,' 'Medium,' and 'Inferior' sacrifices, including animals, silk, grain, jade, and so on. Panegyrics were sung, and robes of proper colour worn. In spring, summer season, fall, and winter there were the seasonal sacrifices at the suitable altars. Taoism and Buddhism had their temples, monasteries, priests, sacrifices, and routine; and there were village and wayside temples and shrines to forefathers, the gods of thunder, rain, wind, grain, farming, and many others. Now encouraged, now tolerated, now persecuted, the ecclesiastical personnel and structure of Taoism and Buddhism endured into contemporary times, when we find complete plans of ecclesiastical gradations of rank and authority implanted upon these two priestly hierarchies, and their temples, priests, etc., satisfying typically, with worship of forefathers, State or official (Confucianism) and personal or informal, and the observance of various annual celebrations, like 'All Souls' Day' for roaming and starving ghosts, the spiritual requirements of the people as the 'Three Faiths' (San Chiao). The emperor, as high priest, took the duty for calamities, and so on, making confession to Paradise and hoping that as a punishment the wicked be diverted from the people to his own person. Statesmen, nobles, and authorities discharged, as already kept in mind, priestly functions in connexion with the State faith in addition to their normal duties. As a rule, priests correct, frowned upon as non-producers, were hired from the lower classes, were celibate, unintellectual, idle, and immoral. There was absolutely nothing, even in the fancy ceremonies on unique occasions in the Buddhist temples, which could be likened to what is referred to as 'public worship' and 'common prayer' in the West. Praise had for its sole object either the attainment of some great or the avoidance of some evil.

Normally this represents the state of things under the Republican régime; the chief differences being greater overlook of ecclesiastical matters and the conversion of a great deal of temples into schools.

Professional Institutions
We read of doctors, blind musical artists, poets, instructors, prayer-makers, designers, scribes, painters, diviners, ceremonialists, orators, and other ones throughout the Feudal Duration, These professions were of ecclesiastical beginning, not yet entirely separated from the 'Church,' and both in earlier and later times not always or typically differentiated from one another. Hence the historiographers combined the duties of statesmen, scholars, authors, and generals. The professions of authors and instructors, musicians and poets, were united in someone. And so it continued to the present day. Priests release medical functions, poets still sing their verses. But skilled medical experts, though couple of, are to be found, as well as women physicians; there are veterinary cosmetic surgeons, musicians (mainly belonging to the poorest classes and

usually blind), actors, instructors, attorneys, diviners, artists, letter-writers, and lots of others, men of letters being perhaps the most popular and most esteemed.

Accessory Institutions
A system of schools, academies, colleges, and universities gotten in towns, districts, departments, and principalities. The direction was divided into 'Main Learning' and 'Great Learning.' There were unique schools of dancing and music. Libraries and almshouses for old guys are discussed. Associations of academics for literary functions appear to have been many.

Whatever form and direction education might have taken, it became stereotyped at an early age by the roadway to office being made to lead through a knowledge of the classical writings of the age-old sages. It ended up being not only 'the thing' to be well versed in the phrases of Confucius, Mencius; and so on, and to be able to compose great essays on them including not a single mistakenly written character, but worthless for aspirants to office-- who constituted practically the whole of the literary class-- to acquire any other knowledge. So consumed was the national mind by this literary mania that even babies' spines were made to bend so as to produce when adult the 'academic stoop.' And from the simple fact that besides the academic class the remainder of the community included agriculturists, craftsmens, and merchants, whose knowledge was that of their fathers and grandpas, inculcated in the sons and grand sons as it had been in them, showing them how to continue in the exact same groove the calling to which Fate had assigned them, a departure from which would have been thought about 'unfilial'-- unless, naturally (as it extremely rarely did), it went the length of achieving through research study of the classics a location in the main class, and hence shedding eternal lustre on the family-- it will easily be seen that there was absolutely nothing to trigger education to be concerned with any but one or two of the subjects which are included by Western peoples under that classification. It ended up being at an early age, and remained for lots of centuries, a rote-learning of the elementary text-books, followed by a similar acquisition by heart of the texts of the works of Confucius and other classical authors. And so it remained till the abolition, in 1905, of the old competitive evaluation system, and the replacement of all that is included in the term 'modern education' at schools, colleges, and universities all over the nation, in which there is rapidly growing up a force that is regenerating the Chinese people, and will make itself felt throughout the entire world.

It is this keen and shrewd gratitude of the learned, and this desire for knowledge, which, disallowing the catastrophe of foreign domination, will make China, in the truest and best sense of the word, a great country, where, as in the United States of America, the rigid class status and undervaluation, if not disdaining, of knowledge which are showing so dreadful in England and other European countries will be kept away from, and the upper class of learning established in its place.

Besides educational institutions, we find organizations for poor relief, health centers, foundling healthcare facilities, orphan asylums, banking, insurance, and loan associations, visitors' clubs, mercantile corporations, anti-opium societies, co-operative burial societies, along with a lot of others, some mimicked from Western models.

Physical Mutilations

Compared with the practices found to exist among most primitive races, the mutilations the Chinese were in the practice of inflicting were but few. They flattened the skulls of their children by methods of stones, so as to cause them to taper at the top, and we have already seen what they did to their spinal columns; also the mutilations in warfare, and the penalties caused both within and without the law; and how filial kids and loyal spouses mutilated themselves for the sake of their mother and father and to prevent remarriage. Eunuchs, obviously, existed in great numbers. People bit, cut, or marked their arms to pledge oaths. However the practices which are more peculiarly related to the Chinese are the compressing of women's feet and the wearing of the line, misnamed 'pigtail.' The former is known to have been in force about A.D. 934, though it may have been introduced as early as 583. It did not, however, become strongly developed for more than a century. This 'very unpleasant mutilation,' started in infancy, illustrates the tyranny of style, for it is supposed to have arisen in the imitation by the women usually of the small feet of a royal courtesan appreciated by among the emperors from ten to fifteen centuries ago (the books vary regarding his identity). The second was a badge of bondage inflicted by the Manchus on the Chinese when they dominated China at the beginning of the seventeenth century. Discountenanced by governmental orders, both of these practices are now tending toward extinction, however, obviously, compressed feet and 'pigtails' are still to be seen in every town and village. Legally, the line was eliminated when the Chinese rid themselves of the Manchu yoke in 1912.

Funeral Rites

Not comprehending the real nature of death, the Chinese believed it was merely a state of suspended animation, in which the soul had couldn't go back to the body, though it may yet do so, even after long intervals. Subsequently they postponed burial, and fed the dead body, and went on to the house-tops and called aloud to the spirit to return. When at length they were convinced that the absent spirit could not be caused to return to the body, they put the latter in a coffin and buried it-- offering it, however, with all that it had found essential in this life (food, clothes, spouses, servants, and so on), which it would require also in the next (in their view rather a continuation of the present presence than the start of another)-- and, having inducted or persuaded the spirit to get in the 'soul-tablet' which accompanied the funeral procession (which took place the moment the tablet was 'dotted,' i.e. when the character wang, 'prince,' was become chu, 'lord'), carried it back home again, set it up in a shrine in the main hall, and fell down and worshipped it. Hence was the spirit propitiated, and as long as occasional offerings were not ignored the power for evil possessed by it would not be exerted against the making it through inmates of the home, whom it had so thoughtlessly deserted.

The latter grieved by yelling, wailing, marking their feet, and beating their boobs, renouncing (in the earliest times) even their outfits, residence, and valuables to the dead, getting rid of to mourning-sheds of clay, fasting, or eating only rice gruel, sleeping on straw with a clod for a pillow, and speaking only on subjects of death and burial. Office and public duties were resigned, and marital relationship, music, and separation from the clan restricted.

During the lapse of the long ages of monarchical rule funeral service rites became more fancy and splendid, but, though less rigid and ceremonious since the organization of the Republic, they have maintained their important character down to the present day.

Funeral ceremonial was more exacting than that connected with the majority of other observances, including those of marriage. Invitations or alerts were sent to good friends, and after receipt of these fu, on the numerous days selected therein, the visitor was obliged to send presents, just like money, paper horses, servants, and so on, and go and take part the lamentations of the hired mourners and attend at the prayers recited by the priests. Funeral etiquette could not be pu 'd, i.e. made good, if overlooked or disregarded at the right time, as it could in the case of the marriage ritualistic.

Rather than symmetrical public graveyards, as in the West, the Chinese cemeteries belong to the family or clan of the departed, and are normally lovely and serene places planted with trees and surrounded by creative walls enclosing the grave-mounds and huge tablets. The cemeteries themselves are the metonyms of the towns, and the graves of the houses. In the north particularly the tomb is really typically surmounted by a huge marble tortoise bearing the inscribed tablet, or what we call the gravestone, on its back. The tombs of the last 2 lines of emperors, the Ming and the Manchu, are magnificent structures, topped huge areas, and always creatively situated on hillsides facing natural or artificial lakes or seas. Contrary to the practice in Egypt, with the two exceptions above pointed out the dominating dynasties have always damaged the burial places of their predecessors. But for this savage vandalism, China would most likely possess the most spectacular assembly of royal burial places worldwide's records.

Laws of Customs
Throughout the entire course of their existence as a social aggregate the Chinese have pushed ritualistic observances to an extreme limitation. "Events," says the Li chi, the great classic of ceremonial uses, "are the best of all things by which men live." Ranks were distinguished by different headdresses, garments, badges, weapons, writing-tablets, number of attendants, carriages, horses, height of walls, etc. Daily as well as official life was regulated by minute observances. There were written codes embracing practically every attitude and act of inferiors towards superiors, of superiors towards inferiors, and of equates to towards equates to. Visits, types of address, and giving of presents had each their set of solutions, known and observed by each as strictly and regularly as each kid in China learned by heart and repeated aloud the three-word sentences of the elementary Trimetrical Timeless. But while the school text-book was extremely basic, ceremonial observances were exceptionally sophisticated. A Chinese was in this respect as much a slave to the living as in his funeral rites he was a servant to the dead. Only now, in the rush of 'modern-day progress,' is the doffing of the hat replacing the 'kowtow' (k'o-t'ou).

It is in this matter of ceremonial observances that the East and the West have misconstrued one another maybe more than in all other ones. Where rules of etiquette are not only different, but are diametrically opposed, there is every chance for misconception, if not estrangement. The points at problem in such questions as 'kowtowing' to the emperor and the worshipping of ancestors are normally known, but the Westerner, as a rule, is oblivious of the simple fact that if he wishes to conform to Chinese rules when in China (rather than to those Western customs which are in tons of cases regrettably taking their place) he should not, for example, take off his hat when entering a house or a temple, should not shake hands with his host, nor, if he wants to express approval, should he clap his hands. Clapping of hands in China (i.e. non-Europeanized China) is used to repel the sha ch'i, or deathly impact of evil spirits, and to clap the hands at the close of the remarks of a Chinese host (as I have seen prominent, well-meaning, but ill-guided guys of the West do) is comparable to disapproval, if not insult. Had our diplomatists been sociologists instead of only industrial representatives, more than one war may have been avoided.

Practices and Customs
At periods throughout the year the Chinese make holiday. Their public festivals begin with the celebration of the introduction of the new year. They let off innumerable firecrackers, and make much merrymaking in their homes, drinking and feasting, and visiting their good friends for some days. Accounts are squared, homes cleaned, fresh paper 'door-gods' pasted on the front doors, strips of red paper with characters suggesting happiness, wealth, good luck, durability, etc., stuck on the doorposts or the lintel, tables, and so on, covered with red cloth, and flowers and decorations displayed all over. Business is suspended, and the joviality, wearing new clothes, feasting, going to, offerings to gods and ancestors, and idling continue quite regularly during the first half of the very first moon, the getaway ending with the Banquet of Lanterns, which inhabits the last 3 days. It came from the Han dynasty 2000 years ago. Numerous lanterns of all sizes, shapes, colours (except wholly white, or rather undyed material, the colour of mourning), and designs are lit in front of public and private structures, but making use of these was an addition about 800 years later, i.e. about 1200 years ago. Paper dragons, hundreds of yards long, are moved along the streets at a slow pace, supported on the heads of men whose legs only show up, giving the impression of huge snakes winding through the roads.

Of the other primary celebrations, about 8 in number (not counting the celebrations of the 4 times with their equinoxes and solstices), four are specifically interested in the propitiation of the spirits-- particularly, the Earlier Spirit Celebration (fifteenth day of second moon), the Festival of the Tombs (about the 3rd day of the third moon), when graves are put in order and special offerings made to the dead, the Middle Spirit Celebration (fifteenth day of seventh moon), and the Later Spirit Festival (fifteenth day of tenth moon). The Dragon-boat Celebration (fifth day of fifth moon) is said to have stemmed as a celebration of the death of the poet Ch' ü Yüan, who drowned himself in disgust at the main intrigue and corruption of which he was the victim, but the thing is the procuring of adequate rain to make sure a good harvest. It is celebrated by racing with long narrow boats shaped to represent dragons and propelled by scores of rowers, pasting of charms on the doors of houses, and eating a unique kind of rice-cake, with an alcohol as a beverage.

Chapter 6: Spirits and Habits

The Spirit That Clears the Way

The fifteenth day of the eighth moon is the Mid-autumn Celebration, understood by immigrants as All Souls' Day. On this occasion the women praise the moon, offering cakes, fruit, etc. The gateways of Purgatory are opened, and the hungry ghosts troop forth to enjoy themselves for a month on the good things provided for them by the pious. The ninth day of the ninth moon is the Chung Yang Celebration, when every one who possibly can ascends to a high place-- a hill or temple-tower. This inaugurates the kite-flying season and is supposed to promote longevity. During that season, which lasts some months, the Chinese people the sky with dragons, centipedes, frogs, butterflies, and hundreds of other cleverly devised beings, which, by means of basic mechanisms worked by the wind, roll their eyes, make suitable noises, and move their paws, wings, tails, etc., in a most sensible manner. The festival originated in a caution gotten by a scholar called Huan Ching from his master Fei Ch' ang-fang, a local of Ju-nan in Honan, who lived during the Han dynasty, that a terrible calamity was about to happen, and enjoining him to leave with his family to a high place. On his return he found all his domestic animals dead, and was told that they had died rather than himself and his family members. On New Year's Eve (Tuan Nien or Chu Hsi) the Kitchen-god ascends to Heaven to make his yearly report, the wise feasting him with honey and other sticky food right before his departure, so that his lips might be sealed and he be unable to 'let on' too much to the powers that be in the regions above!

Sports and Games

The first sports of the Chinese were festival gatherings for functions of archery, to which had a lot of success exercises partaking of a army character. Searching was a preferred amusement. They played games of computation, chess (or the 'game of war'), shuttlecock with the feet, pitch-pot (tossing arrows from some distance into a narrow-necked jar), and 'horn-goring' (battling on the shoulders of others with horned masks on their heads). Stilts, football, dice-throwing, boat-racing, dog-racing, cock-fighting, kite-flying, along with singing and dancing marionettes, afforded leisure and amusement.

A lot of these games ended up being obsolete in course of time, and brand-new ones were created. At the end of the Monarchical Period, throughout the Manchu dynasty, we find those most in usage to be foot-shuttlecock, lifting of beams headed with heavy stones-- dumb-bells four feet long and weighing thirty or forty pounds-- kite-flying, quail-fighting, cricket-fighting, sending birds after seeds tossed into the air, roaming through fields, playing chess or 'morra,' or gambling with cards, dice, or over the cricket- and quail-fights or seed-catching birds. There were numerous and varied kids's games tending to develop strength, ability, quickness of action, adult impulse, precision, and sagacity. Theatricals were performed by walking performers on stages put up opposite temples, though long-term theatres also existed, female parts until recently being taken by male stars. Peep-shows, magicians, ventriloquists, acrobats, fortune-tellers, and story-tellers kept crowds entertained or interested. Usually, 'young China' of the present day, related to the party of progress, seems to have adopted the majority of the outside but extremely few of the indoor games of Western countries.

Domestic Life

In domestic or personal life, observances at birth, betrothal, and marital relationship were sophisticated, and maintained superstitious aspects. Early rising was general. Shaving of the head and beard, as well as cleansing of the ears and massage, was done by barbers. There were public baths in all cities and towns. Shops were closed at nightfall, and, the streets being till current times ill-lit or dark, guests or their attendants brought lanterns. A lot of homes, except the poorest, had private watchmen. Usually two meals a day were taken. Dinners to good friends were served at inns or dining establishments, accompanied or followed by musical or theatrical performances. The place of honour is specified in Western books on China to be on the left, but the fact is that the place of honour is the one which shows the utmost solicitude for the security of the guest. It is therefore not always one fixed place, but would generally be the one facing the door, so that the visitor might be in a position to see an opponent get in, and take measures appropriately.

Lap-dogs and cage-birds were kept as pets; 'wonks,' the huang kou, or 'yellow dog,' were guards of homes and street scavengers. Aquaria with goldfish were usually to be seen in the houses of the upper and middle classes, the gardens and courtyards of which usually contained rockeries and creative shrubs and flowers.

Hairs were never ever used, and moustaches and beards only after forty, before which age the hair grew, if at all, very scantily. Full, thick beards, as in the West, were practically never ever seen, even on the aged. Snuff-bottles, tobacco-pipes, and fans were brought by both sexes. Nails were used long by members of the literary and leisured classes. Non-Manchu ladies and girls had cramped feet, and both Manchu and Chinese ladies used cosmetics easily.

Industrial Institutions

While the guys addressed farm-work, ladies looked after the mulberry-orchards and silkworms, and did spinning, weaving, and embroidery. This, the primitive department of labour, held throughout, though added to on both sides, so that eventually the men did most of the farming, arts, production, circulation, battling, and so on, and the women, besides the duties above named and some field-labour, mended old clothes, drilled and sharpened needles, pasted tin-foil, made shoes, and gathered and arranged the leaves of the tea-plant. In course of time trades became highly specialized-- their number being legion-- and localized, bankers, for instance, gathering together in Shansi, carpenters in Chi Chou, and porcelain-manufacturers in Jao Chou, in Kiangsi.

Regarding land, it became at an early age the property of the sovereign, who grown it out to his family members or favourites. It was arranged on the ching, or 'well' system-- 8 personal squares round a ninth public square cultivated by the 8 farmer families in common for the advantage of the State. From the starting to the end of the Monarchical Period tenure went on to be of the Crown, land being unallodial, and mainly kept in clans or families, and not entailed, the conditions of period being payment of an annual tax, a fee for alienation, and cash compensation for individual services to the Government, usually incorporated into the direct tax as scutage. Slavery, unidentified in the earliest times, existed as an acknowledged organization throughout the entire of the Monarchical Duration.

Production was chiefly confined to human and animal labour, equipment being only now in use on a large scale. Internal circulation was carried on from numerous centres and at fairs, stores, markets, etc. With few exceptions, the great trade-routes by land and sea have remained the same during the last two 1,000 years. Foreign trade was with Western Asia, Greece, Rome, Carthage, Arabia, and so on, and from the seventeenth century A.D. more normally with European nations. The typical primitive methods of conveyance, like human beings, animals, carts, boats, and so on, were partially displaced by steam-vessels from 1861 onward.

Exchange was affected by barter, cowries of different values being the prototype of coins, which were cast in greater or less amount under each reign. But till within current years there was only one coin, the copper money, in use, bullion and paper notes being the other media of exchange. Silver Mexican dollars and subsidiary coins entered into use with the introduction of foreign commerce. Weights and steps (which normally decreased from north to south), formally set up partly on the decimal system, were discarded by the people in normal business deals for the easier duodecimal neighborhood.

Arts
Searching, fishing, cooking, weaving, coloring, carpentry, metallurgy, glass-, brick-, and paper-making, printing, and book-binding were in a more or less primitive phase, the mechanical arts showing much servile imitation and simpleness in design; but pottery, carving, and lacquer-work were in an extremely high state of development, the articles produced being gone beyond in quality and charm by no other ones worldwide.

Farming and Rearing of Livestock
From the earliest times the greater part of the available land was under growing. Other than when the country has been devastated by war, the Chinese have dedicated close attention to the growing of the dirt continuously for forty centuries. Even the hills are terraced for extra growing room. However, hardship and governmental inaction triggered much to lie idle. There were 2 yearly crops in the north, and 5 in two years in the south. Maybe two-thirds of the population cultivated the dirt. The methods, though, remained primitive; but the great fertility of the ground and the great market of the farmer, with generous but cautious use of fertilizers, made it possible for the vast territory to support an enormous population. Rice, wheat, barley, buckwheat, maize, kaoliang, several millets, and oats were the chief grains cultivated. Beans, peas, oil-bearing seeds (sesame, rape, etc.), fibre-plants (hemp, ramie, jute, cotton, etc.), starch-roots (taros, yams, sweet potatoes, etc.), tobacco, indigo, tea, sugar, fruits, were amongst the more crucial crops produced. Fruit-growing, however, lacked scientific approach. The rotation of crops was not an usual practice, but grafting, pruning, dwarfing, enlarging, selecting, and differing species were well comprehended. Vegetable-culture had reached a high state of perfection, the tiniest spots of land being made to produce perfectly. This is the more

creditable inasmuch as a lot of small farmers could not afford to acquire expensive foreign machinery, which, in many cases, would be too large or complicated for their functions.

The principal animals, birds, etc., reared were the pig, ass, horse, mule, cow, sheep, goat, buffalo, yak, fowl, duck, goose, pigeon, silkworm, and bee.

The Ministry of Agriculture and Commerce, the successor to the Board of Agriculture, Produces, and Commerce, set up throughout recent years, is now adapting Western techniques to the growing of the fertile soil of China, and even greater results than in the past may be expected in the future.

Sentiments and Moral Ideas
The Chinese have always shown an eager enjoy the stunning-- in flowers, music, poetry, literature, embroidery, paintings, porcelain. They cultivated decorative plants, practically every house, as we saw, having its garden, big or small, and tables were often embellished with flowers in vases or decorative wire baskets or fruits or sweetmeats. Confucius made music an instrument of federal government. Paper bearing the written character was so appreciated that it might not be thrown on the ground or trodden on. Pleasure was always displayed in beautiful scenery or tales of the wonderful. Commanding or agreeable situations were chosen for temples. But till within the last few years streets and houses were usually unclean, and decency in public frequently absent.

Morality was favoured by public opinion, but in spite of early marital relationships and concubinage there was much laxity. Cruelty both to humans and animals has always been a significant quality in the Chinese character. Savagery in warfare, cannibalism, luxury, drunkenness, and corruption dominated in the earliest times. The mindset towards women was despotic. But moral principles pervaded the classical writings and formed the basis of law. Despite these, the inferior belief of revenge was, as we have seen, authorized and preached as a sacred duty. As a result of the universal yin-yang dualistic doctrines, immorality was leniently concerned. In contemporary times, at least, mercantile honour was high, "a merchant's word is as good as his bond" being truer in China than in many other nations. Intemperance was uncommon. Opium-smoking was much enjoyed till making use of the drug was by force repressed (1906-- 16). Even now much is smuggled into the country, or its development neglected by paid off authorities. Clan quarrels and battles prevailed, vendettas sometimes continuing for generations. Suicide under depressing situations was approved and honoured; it was regularly resorted to under the sting of great oppression. There was a deep respect for parents and superiors. Disregard of the truth, when useful, was universal, and unattended by a sense of pity, even on detection. Thieving was common. The illegal exactions of rulers were difficult. In times of prosperity pride and fulfillment in material matters was not hidden, and was typically short-sighted. Politeness was virtually universal, though said to be often shallow; but gratitude was a marked particular, and was heartfelt. Shared conjugal affection was strong. The love of gaming was universal.

But little has taken place recently to modify the above characters. However the inferior traits are certainly being changed by education and by the formation of societies whose members bind themselves against immorality, concubinage, gaming, drinking, smoking, etc.

Religious Ideas Chinese religion is inherently a mindset towards the spirits or gods with the thing of acquiring a benefit or averting a calamity. We shall handle it more fully in another chapter. Suffice it to say here that it came from ancestor-worship, and that the majority of it remains ancestor-worship to the present day. The State religious belief, which was Confucianism, was ancestor-worship. Taoism, originally an approach, became a worship of spirits-- of the living souls of dead guys supposed to have used up their residence in animals, reptiles, bugs, trees, stones, and so on-- borrowed the cape of religious belief from Buddhism, which eventually outshone it, and deteriorated into a system of exorcism and magic. Buddhism, a faith coming from India, in which Buddha, once a man, is worshipped, in which no beings are known with greater power than can be attained to by man, and according to which at death the soul migrates into anything from a deified human being to an elephant, a bird, a plant, a wall, a broom, or any piece of inorganic matter, was imported all set made into China and took the side of popular superstition and Taoism against the orthodox belief, finding that its power lay in the impact on the popular mind of its doctrine respecting a future state, in contrast to the indifference of Confucianism. Its pleading for empathy and preservation of life met a sobbing need, and but for it the state of things in this respect would be worse than it is.

Religion, apart from ancestor-worship, does not go into largely into Chinese life. There is none of the real 'love of God' found, for instance, in the impassioned as distinguished from the standard Christian. And as ancestor-worship slowly loses its hold and dies out agnosticism will take its spot.

Superstitions A practically unlimited variety of superstitious practices, because of the belief in the great or evil impacts of departed spirits, exists in all parts of China. Days are fortunate or unlucky. Eclipses are because of a dragon attempting to eat the sun or the moon. The rainbow is supposed to be the result of a conference between the impure vapours of the sun and the earth. Amulets are used, and appeals hung up, sprigs of artemisia or of peach-blossom are positioned near beds and over lintels respectively, children and adults are 'locked to life' by means of locks on chains or cords worn round the neck, old brass mirrors are supposed to cure madness, figures of gourds, tigers' claws, or the unicorn are used to guarantee good fortune or ward off sickness, fire, etc., spells of tons of kinds, composed mainly of the written characters for joy and durability, are used, or written on paper, cloth, leaves, and so on, and burned, the ashes being made into a decoction and intoxicated by the young or sick.

Divination by methods of the divining stalks (the divining plant, milfoil or yarrow) and the tortoiseshell has been carried on from time immemorial, but was not originally practiced with the thing of ascertaining future events, but in order to decide doubts, much as lots are drawn or a coin tossed in the West. Fêng-shui, "the art of adapting the residence of the living and the dead so as to co-operate and harmonize with the regional currents of the cosmic breath" a doctrine which had its root in ancestor-worship, has exercised a massive impact on Chinese idea and life from the earliest times, and particularly from those of Chu Hsi and other philosophers of the Sung dynasty.

Knowledge

Having actually kept in mind that Chinese education was primarily literary, and why it was so, it is simple to see that there would be little or no need for the kind of knowledge classified in the West under the head of science. In up until now as any need existed, it did so, at any rate in the beginning, only since it subserved crucial needs. Therefore, astronomy, or more appropriately astrology, was studied in order that the calendar may be controlled, and so the routine of agriculture correctly followed, for on that depended the people's everyday rice, or rather, in the start, the different fruits and types of flesh which constituted their means of sustentation before their now universal food was understood. In philosophy they have had 2 durations of great activity, the very first start with Lao Tzŭ and Confucius in the 6th century B.C. and ending with the Burning of the Books by the First Emperor, Shih Huang Ti, in 213 B.C.; the second beginning with Chou Tzŭ (A.D. 1017-- 73) and ending with Chu Hsi (1130-- 1200). The department of approach in the imperial library consisted of in 190 B.C. 2705 volumes by 137 authors. There can be no doubt that this zeal for the orthodox learning, integrated with the literary test for office, was the reason scientific knowledge was stopped from developing; so much so, that after four thousand or more years of nationwide life we find, throughout the Manchu Duration, which ended the monarchical régime, few of the informed class, giants though they were in knowledge of all departments of their literature and history (the continuity of their traditions laid down in their twenty-four Dynastic Annals has been referred to as among the great wonders of the world), with even the elementary clinical learning of a schoolboy in the West. 'Crude,' 'primitive,' 'average,' 'vague,' 'inaccurate,' 'want of analysis and generalization,' are terms we find applied to their knowledge of such leading sciences as geography, mathematics, chemistry, botany, and geology. Their medicine was much obstructed by superstitious notion, and maybe more so by such beliefs as that the seat of the intelligence is in the stomach, that thoughts follow the heart, that the pit of the stomach is the seat of the breath, that the soul lives in the liver, and so on-- the outcome partially of the idea that dissection of the body would maim it permanently during its presence in the Otherworld. What development was made was due to European instruction; and this again is the causa causans of the great wave of development in clinical and philosophical knowledge which is rolling over the entire country and will have marked effects on the history of the world throughout the coming century.

Language

Initially polysyllabic, the Chinese language later presumed a monosyllabic, separating, uninflected form, grammatical relations being shown by position. From the earliest forms of speech some secondary vernacular languages emerged in different districts, and from these sprang regional dialects, and so on. Tone-distinctions emerged-- i.e. the same words pronounced with a different intonation came to mean different things. Development of these distinctions resulted in carelessness of articulation, and multiplication of what would be homonyms but for these tones. It is inaccurate to assume that the tones were invented to distinguish comparable sounds. So that, at the present day, anybody who says ma will mean either an exclamation, hemp, horse, or curse according to the quality he offers to the sound. The language remains in a primitive state, without inflexion, declension, or distinction of parts of speech. The order in a sentence is: subject, verb, complement direct, enhance indirect. Gender is formed by unique particles; number by prefixing characters, and so on; cases by position or proper prepositions. Adjectives precede nouns; position identifies contrast; and absence of punctuation causes obscurity. The latter is now introduced into a lot of freshly published works. The new education is bringing with it many words and expressions not found in the old literature or dictionaries. Japanese idioms which are now being imported into the language are making it less pure.

The written language, too well known to really need in-depth description, a thing of appeal and a joy for ever to those able to appreciate it, said to have taken initially the form of knotted cables and then of notches on wood (though this was more probably the beginning of numeration than of writing appropriate), took later that of disrespectful outlines of natural items, and then went on to the phonetic system, under which each character is composed of two parts, the radical, showing the meaning, and the phonetic, indicating the sound. They were symbols, non-agglutinative and non-inflexional, and were written in vertical columns, most likely from having in early times been painted or cut on strips of bark.

Achievements of the Chinese
As the result of all this fitful fever during so many centuries, we find that the Chinese, after having actually lived in nests "in order to keep away from the animals," and then in caves, have built themselves houses and palaces which are still made after the pattern of their prototype, with a flat wall behind, the openings in front, the walls put in after the pillars and roof-tree have been repaired, and out-buildings added on as side extensions. The k' ang, or 'stove-bed' (now a platform made of bricks), found all over the northern provinces, was a location dug of the side of the cave, with an opening underneath in which (as now) a fire was lit in winter. Windows and shutters opened upward, being a survival of the mat or shade hung in front of the apertures in the walls of the primitive cave-dwelling. 4 of these structures dealing with each other round a square made the yard, and one or more courtyards made the compound. They have fed themselves on almost every little thing edible to be found on, under, or above land or water, except milk, but live primarily on rice, chicken, fish, vegetables, consisting of garlic, and tea, though at one time they ate flesh and drank wine, sometimes to excess, right before tea was cultivated. They have dressed themselves in skins and feathers, and then in silks and satins, but primarily in cotton, and hardly ever in wool. Under the Manchu régime the kind of dress adopted was that of this horse-riding race, demonstrating the chief attributes of that honorable animal, the broad sleeves representing the hoofs, the queue the mane, etc. This line was formed of the hair growing from the back part of the scalp, the front of which was shaved. Unlike the Egyptians, they did not wear wigs. They have almost always had the decency to wear their coats long, and have despised the Westerner for wearing his too short. They are now paradoxical enough to make the error of adopting the Westerner's costume.

They have made to themselves great canals, bridges, aqueducts, and the longest wall there has ever been on the face of the earth (which could not be seen from the moon, as some sinologists have mistakenly presumed, any more than a hair, however long, could be seen at a short distance of a hundred yards). They have made long and broad roads, but couldn't keep them in repair work throughout the last few centuries, however much zeal, potentially because of commerce on oil- or electricity-driven wheels, is now being shown in this direction. They have built honorary portals to chaste widows, pagodas, and arched bridges of great beauty, not forgetting to surround each city with a high and substantial wall to stay out hostile people. They have made many implements and weapons, from pens and fans and chopsticks to ploughs and carts and ships; from fiery darts, 'flame elephants,' bows and spears, spiked chariots, battering-rams, and hurling-engines to mangonels, trebuchets, matchlocks of wrought iron and plain bore with long barrels resting on a stock, and gingals fourteen feet long resting on a tripod, cuirasses of quilted cotton cloth covered with brass knobs, and helmets of iron or polished steel, sometimes inlaid, with neck- and ear-lappets. And they have been content not to surpass these to any considerable level; but have lately shown a propensity to make the later patterns imported from the West in their own factories.

They have produced among the greatest and most remarkable build-ups of literature the world has ever seen, and the finest porcelain; some music, not very fine; and some magnificent painting, though barely any sculpture, and little architecture that will live.

Chapter 7: Background of the Mythology

Folklore and Intellectual Development
The Manichæst, yin-yang (dualist), idea of presence, to which further recommendation will be made in the next chapter, finds its illustration in the double life, real and fictional, of all the peoples of the earth. They have both real histories and mythological histories. In the preceding chapter I have dealt briefly with the very first-- the life of reality-- in China from the earliest times to the present day; the succeeding chapters are interested in the second-- the life of creativity. A survey of the first was required for a total grasp of the 2nd. The 2 respond upon one another, affecting the nationwide character and through it the history of the world.

Folklore is the science of the unscientific man's clarification of what we call the Otherworld-- itself and its citizens, their mysterious habits and surprising actions both there and here, generally including the creation of the world also. By the Otherworld he does not always mean anything remote or perhaps invisible, though the things he explains would mostly be included by us under those terms. In some countries myths are plentiful, in others limited. Why should this be? Why should some peoples tell a lot of and marvellous tales about their gods and other ones say little about them, though they may say a great deal to them? We remember the 'great' myths of Greece and Scandinavia. Other races are 'poor' in myths. The difference is to be clarified by the psychological characters of the peoples as moulded by their environments and hereditary propensities. The issue is naturally a mental one, for it is, as already kept in mind, in creativity that myths have their root. Now creativity grows with each stage of intellectual progress, for intellectual development indicates increasing representativeness of thought. In the lower phases of human development imagination is weak and ineffective; in the greatest phases it is strong and positive.

The Chinese Intelligence
The Chinese are not unimaginative, but their minds did not go on to the construction of any myths which should be world-great and immortal; and one reason that they did not construct such myths was that their intellectual development was arrested at a relatively early phase. It was jailed since there was not that contact and competitors with other tribes which demands brain-work of an active kind as the option of subjugation, inferiority, or extinction, and because, as we have already seen, the knowledge needed of them was primarily the parrot-like repetition of the old rather than the thinking-out of the new1-- a state of things rendered possible by the seclusion just described. Confucius discountenanced conversation about the super, and just as it is probable that the admonitions of Wên Wang, the virtual creator of the Chou dynasty (1121-- 255 B.C.), against drunkenness, in a time right before tea was understood to them, helped to make the Chinese the sober people that they are, so it is likely-- more than probable-- that this attitude of Confucius may have nipped in the bud much that might have developed an energetic mythology, though for a factor to be mentioned later it might be doubted if he thus deprived the world of any gorgeous and marvellous actual results of the highest flights of poetical creativity. There are times, like those of any great political turmoil, when human nature will assert itself and break through its shackles in spite of all artificial or

conventional restraints. Considering the massive impact of Confucianism throughout the latter half of Chinese history-- i.e. the last two 1000 years-- it is unexpected that the Chinese attempted to think of supernatural matters at all, except in the matter of propitiating their dead forefathers. That they did so is evidence not only of humanity's intrinsic propensity to tell stories, but also of the irrepressible strength of sensation which breaks all laws and rules under great stimulus. On the opposing unæsthetic side this might be compared to the feeling which prompts the unpremeditated assassination of a man who is guilty of great oppression, despite the fact that it be certain that in due course he would have met his deserts at the hands of the general public executioner.

The Influence of Faith
Apart from this, the impact of Confucianism would have been even greater than it was, but for the royal partiality periodically revealed for rival teachings, just like Buddhism and Taoism, which tossed their weight on the side of the superhuman, and which sometimes were exalted to such great heights regarding be formally acknowledged as State religious beliefs. These, Buddhism especially, interested the popular imagination and love of the wonderful. Buddhism mentioned the future state and the nature of the gods in no unpredictable tones. It showed men how to reach the one and get to the other. Its founder was virtuous; his commandments pure and life-sustaining. It provided in great part what Confucianism did not have. And, as in the fifth and 6th centuries A.D., when Buddhism and Taoism joined forces and a working union existed between them, they practically excluded for the time all the "chilly development of Confucian classicism."

Other opponents of myth, consisting of a vital thinker of great ability, we will have event to see currently.

History and Myth
The sobriety and precision of Chinese historians is common. I have dilated upon this in another work, and really need include here only what I accidentally omitted there-- a point hitherto unnoticed or at least unremarked-- that the really word for history in Chinese (shih) means impartiality or an unbiased annalist. It has been said that where there is much myth there is little history, and vice versa, and though this may not be universally true, undoubtedly the persistently genuine recording of realities, events, and phrases, even at the danger of loss, yea, and actual death of the historian as the outcome of his refusal to make incorrect entries in his chronicle at the bidding of the emperor (as when it comes to the historiographers of Ch' i in 547 B.C.), suggests a type of mind which would need some very strong stimulus to trigger it to skyrocket very far into the hazy worlds of fanciful creativity.

Chinese Rigidness
A further cause, already hinted at above, for the arrest of intellectual development is to be found in the development of the country in size throughout tons of centuries of isolation from the primary stream of world-civilization, without that increase in heterogeneity which comes from the moulding by forces external to itself. "As iron sharpeneth iron, so a man sharpeneth the countenance of his friend." Consequently we find China what is understood to sociology as

an 'aggregate of the very first order,' which during its advancement has parted with its internal life-heat without taking in enough from external sources to enable it to retain the plastic condition required to farther, or at least rapid, development. It is in a state of rigidness, a state recognized and comprehended by the sociologist in his study of the evolution of countries.

The Requirements to Myths

But the mere boost of constructive imagination is not enough to produce myth. If it were, it would be sensible to argue that as intellectual development goes on myths become more numerous, and the greater the development the greater the number of myths. This we do not find. In fact, if constructive imagination went on increasing without the intervention of any further aspect, there need not always be any myth at all. We might almost say that the reverse holds true. We connect myth with primitive folk, not with the best philosophers or the most advanced nations-- not, that is, with the most innovative phases of national development where positive imagination makes the country great and strong. In these phases the philosopher studies or criticizes myth, he does not make it.

In order that there might be myth, three more conditions should be satisfied. There must, as we have seen, be positive imagination, but, nevertheless, there need to not be too much of it. As specified above, mythology, or rather myth, is the unscientific man's clarification. If the useful creativity is so great that it becomes self-critical, if the story-teller doubts his own story, if, in other words, his mind is scientific enough to see that his clarification is no clarification at all, then there can be no myth appropriately so called. As in religious belief, unless the myth-maker believes in his myth with all his heart and soul and strength, and each new disciple, as it is taken care of and grows under his hands throughout the course of years, holds that he must put his shoes from off his feet because the spot whereon he treads is holy ground, the faith will not be propagated, for it will do not have the essential stimulate which alone can make it a living thing.

Stimulus Necessary

The next condition is that there should be a stimulus. It is not ideas, but feelings, which govern the world, and in the history of folklore where sensation is missing we find either weak replica or repeating of the myths of other peoples (though this should not be puzzled with certain aspects which seem to be common to the myths of all races), or mixture, contamination, or "genealogical tree-making," or myths come from by "leisurely, tranquil tradition" and not having the necessary qualities which attract the human soul and make their holders really careful to maintain them amongst their most really loved and valued treasures. But, on the other hand, where sensation is stirred, where the requisite stimulus exists, where the people are in great risk, or attracted by the reward of some out of breath adventure, the contact produces the stimulate of magnificent poetry, the myths have plenty of creative, philosophic, and spiritual suggestiveness, and have abiding relevance and appeal. They are the kids, the poetic fruit, of great labour and serious battles, exposing the most basic forces, hopes, and cravings of the human soul. Nations highly strung, going through difficult emotion, strongly stimulated by constant conflict with other countries, have their creativity stimulated to remarkable poetic creativity. The background of the Danaïds is Egyptian, not Greek, but it was the danger in which the Greeks were put in their wars with the sons of the land of the Pharaohs that stimulated the Greek creativity to the creation of that great myth.

This clarifies why so many of the greatest myths have their staging, not in the nation itself whose valued belongings they are, but where that country is 'playing the great game,' is carrying on wars decisive of significant national events, which excite to the best pitch of enjoyment the feelings both of the contenders and of those who are watching them from their houses. It is by such great events, not by the romance-writer in his tranquil study, that mythology, like literature, is "incisively determined." Imagination, we saw, goes pari passu with intellectual progress, and intellectual progress, in early times, is advanced not so much by the simple contact as by the real dispute of nations. And we see also that myths may, and extremely regularly do, have a character quite different from that of the nation to which they appertain, for environment plays a crucial part both in their beginning and subsequent growth-- a reality too obvious to need in-depth elaboration.

Relentless Soul-expression
A third condition is that the kind of creativity need to be consistent through fairly long periods of time, otherwise not only will there be a lack of sufficient sensation or momentum to trigger the myths to be repeated and kept alive and transmitted to posterity, but the inducement to add to them and so allow them to mature and become complete and rounded off and sufficiently attractive to appeal to the human mind in spite of the foreign character they typically bear will be lacking. To put it simply, myths and legends grow. They resemble not so much the narrative of the story-teller or author as a slowly developing art like music, or a body of ideas like viewpoint. They are human and natural, though they reveal the idea not of any one individual mind, but of the folk-soul, exhibiting in poetical form some great psychological or physiographical truth.

The Character of Chinese Myths
The nature of the case therefore forbids us to expect to find the Chinese myths displaying the advanced state and brilliant heterogeneity of those which have become part of the world's permanent literature. We should expect them to be true to type and conditions, as we expect the other ideas of the Chinese to be, and looking for them in the light of the knowledge we shall find them just where we should expect to find them.

The great legends and eddas exalted among the world's literary masterpieces, and forming part of the very life of a large number of its occupants, are missing in China. "The Chinese people," says one well-known sinologist, "are not prone to mythological creation." "He who expects to find in Tibet," says another author, "the poetical appeal of Greek or Germanic folklore will be dissatisfied. There is a striking hardship of imagination in all the myths and legends. A great uniformity pervades them all. Much of their stories, drawn from the sacred texts, are rather puerile and insipid. It might be kept in mind that the Chinese folklore labours under the same flaw." And then there comes the squashing judgment of an over-zealous Christian missionary sinologist: "There is no hierarchy of gods taken in to rule and populate the world they made, no conclave on Mount Olympus, nor judgment of the mortal soul by Osiris, no transfer of human love and hate, enthusiasms and hopes, to the powers above; all here is credited disembodied firms or principles, and their works are represented as carrying on in quiet order. There is no religion [], no imagination; all is impassible, passionless, dull ... It has not, as in Greece and Egypt, been explained in superb poetry, shadowed forth in gorgeous ritual and stunning festivals, represented in beautiful sculptures, nor preserved in faultless, enforcing fanes and temples, filled with ideal productions." Besides being inaccurate as to tons of its supposed truths, this view would certainly be revealed by further research study to be greatly overemphasized.

Periods Fertile in Myths

What we should expect, then, to find from our philosophical study of the Chinese mind as affected by its surroundings would be barrenness of useful imagination, other than when birth was provided to myth through the operation of some external firm. And this we do find. The period of the defeat of the Yin dynasty and the establishment of the great house of Chou in 1122 B.C., or of the Wars of the 3 States, for example, in the 3rd century after Christ, a time of awful anarchy, a medieval age of legendary heroism, sung in a hundred kinds of prose and verse, which has gotten in as reason into one dozen dramas, or the advent of Buddhism, which opened a brand-new world of idea and life to the easy, sober, peace-loving agricultural folk of China, were stimuli not by any methods lacking result. In China there are gods tons of and heroes tons of, and the really fact of the existence of so great a wide range of gods would realistically indicate a wealth of mythological lore inseparable from their apotheosis. You cannot-- and the Chinese cannot-- get behind reason. A man is not made a god without some cause being assigned for so crucial and far-reaching a big step; and in matters of this sort the stated cause is apt to take the form of a narrative more or less wonderful or amazing. These resulting myths might, naturally, be born and grow at a later time than that in which the situations triggering them occurred, but, if so, that simply proves the persistent power of the coming from stimulus. That in China these stories always or often reach the greatest flights of positive creativity is not kept-- the upkeep of that argument would indeed be inconsistent; but even in those countries where the mythological garden has produced some of the finest flowers countless seeds should have been sown which either did not emerge at all or at least couldn't bring forth fruit. And in the world of mythology it is not only those gods who sit in the greatest seats-- developers of the world or heads of great religions-- who dominate mankind; the humbler, however often no less powerful gods or spirits-- those even who run on all fours and live in holes in the ground, or buzz through the air and have their thrones in the shadow of a leaf-- have usually made a much deeper impress on the minds and in the hearts of the people, and through that impress, for good or evil, have, in greater or less degree, customized the life of the visible universe.

Sources of Chinese Myths

" So, if we ask whence comes the heroic and the romantic, which provides the story-teller's stock-in-trade, the answer is easy. The legends and history of early China furnish abundance of material for them. To the Chinese mind their age-old world was crowded with heroes, fairies, and demons, who played their part in the mixed-up drama, and left a name and popularity both amazing and piquant. Each who recognizes with the methods and the language of the people knows that the country is full of typical challenge which poetic names have been given, and with a lot of them there is associated a legend or a misconception. A deep river's canyon is called 'the Blind Man's Pass,' because a strange little rock, looked at from a certain angle, assumes the summary of the human form, and there becomes linked therewith a pleasing story which reaches its climax in the petrifaction of the hero. A mountain's crest shaped like a stroking eagle will from some one have gotten the name of 'Eagle Mountain,' whilst by its side another formed like a couchant lion will have a name to match. There is no absence of poetry amongst the people, and the majority of striking objects claim a poetic name, and not a few of them are related to curious legends. It is, however, to their nationwide history that the story-teller goes for his most fascinating subjects, and as the so-called history of China imperceptibly passes into the famous period, and this again fades into the legendary, and as all this is assuredly really believed by the masses of the people, it is obvious that in the national life of China there is no dearth of heroes whose deeds of expertise will command the rapt attention of the crowds who listen." 2.

The soul in China is all over in evidence, and if myths have "most importantly to do with the life of the soul" it would appear odd that the Chinese, having spiritualized everything from a stone to the sky, have not been creative of myth. Why they have not the foregoing factors to consider show us clearly enough. We must take them and their myths as we find them. Let us, then, note briefly the outcome of their psychological workings as reacted on by their environment.

Stages of Chinese Myths
We cannot recognize the earliest mythology of the Chinese with that of any primitive race. The myths, if any, of their spot of beginning might have faded and been forgotten in their sluggish migration eastward. We cannot say that when they came from the West (which they most likely did) they brought their myths with them, for in spite of certain conjectural derivations from Babylon we do not find them possessed of any which we can determine as imported by them at that time. But research seems to have gone at least as far as this-- specifically, that while we cannot say that Chinese myth was derived from Indian myth, there is great reason to actually believe that Chinese and Indian myth had a typical origin, which was of course beyond China.

To state in detail the various phases through which Chinese myth has passed would involve a technical description foreign to the purpose of a well-known work. It will sufficiently serve our present purpose to outline its most popular features.

In the earliest times there was an 'age of magic' followed by an 'heroic age,' but myths were very rare right before 800 B.C., and what is called primitive mythology is said to have been developed or mimicked from foreign sources after 820 B.C. In the eighth century B.C. myths of an astrological character began to draw in attention. In the age of Lao Tzŭ (604 B.C.), the reputed founder of the Taoist religion, fresh legends appear, though Lao Tzŭ himself, soaked up in the abstract, records none. Neither did Confucius (551-- 479 B.C.) nor Mencius, who lived two a century later, include any legends to history. However in the Duration of the Warring States (500-- 100 B.C.) fresh stimuli and great feeling triggered to mythological creation.

Tso-ch' iu Ming and Lieh Tzŭ

Tso-ch' iu Ming, analyst on Confucius's Annals, often introduced legend into his history. Lieh Tzŭ (5th and fourth centuries B.C.), a metaphysician, is one of the earliest authors who handle myths. He is the first to discuss the story of Hsi Wang Mu, the Western Queen, and from his day onward the fabulists have vied with one another in great descriptions of the wonders of her fairyland. He was the first to point out the islands of the immortals in the ocean, the kingdoms of the overshadows and giants, the fruit of immortality, the fixing of the paradises by Nü Kua Shih with five-coloured stones, and the great tortoise which supports deep space.

The T'ang and Sung Epochs

Religious love started at this time. The T'ang date (A.B. 618-- 907) was one of the resurrection of the arts of peace after a long period of dissension. A purer and more long-lasting form of intellect was slowly conquering the grosser but less solid superstitious notion. Nevertheless the intellectual movement which now manifested itself was not strong enough to dominate against the powers of mythological darkness. It was reserved for the experts of the Sung Period (A.D. 960-- 1280) to execute to triumph a strong and sustained offensive against the spiritualistic fixations which had weighed upon the Chinese mind more or less constantly from the Han Duration (206 B.C.-A.D. 221) onward. The dogma of materialism was specifically cultivated at this time. The battle of sober reason against superstitious notion or creative creation was mainly a battle of Confucianism against Taoism. Though many centuries had expired since the great Master walked the earth, the anti-myth movement of the T'ang and Sung Periods was in reality the long arm and heavy fist of Confucius stressing a truer rationalism than that of his opponents and denouncing the risk of leaving the firm earth to skyrocket into the unknown hazy areas of fantasy. It was Sung scholarship that gave the death-blow to Chinese mythology.

It is unneeded to labour the point farther, because after the Sung date we do not meet with any period of new mythological creation, and its lack can be ascribed to no other cause than its defeat at the hands of the Sung theorists. After their time the tender plant was always in danger of being stunted or killed by the withering blast of philosophical criticism. Anything in the nature of myth ascribable to post-Sung times can at best be concerned only as a late blossom born when summer days are past.

Myths and Doubt

It will bear repetition to say that unless the myth-builder strongly actually believes in his myth, be he the layer of the foundation-stone or one of the raisers of the superstructure, he will hardly make it a living thing. Once he actually believes in reincarnation and the suspension of natural laws, the limitless vistas of space and the unlimited æons of time are opened to him. He can perform wonders which astonish the world. But if he enable his mind to ask, for instance, why it ought to have been essential for Elijah to part the waters of the Jordan with his garment in order that he and Elisha may pass over dryshod, or for Bodhidharma to stand on a reed to cross the great Yangtzŭ River, or for numerous Immortals to rest on 'favourable clouds' to make their journeys through space, he ruins myth-- his kid is stillborn or does not make it through to maturity. Though the growth of viewpoint and decay of superstition might be good for a nation, the process is definitely conducive to the destruction of its myth and much of its poetry. The real mythologist takes myth for myth, participates in its spirit, and enjoys it.

We may hence expect to find in the world of Chinese mythology a large number of little hills instead of several great mountains, but the little hills are great ones after their kind; and the item of the work is to present Chinese myth as it is, not as it may have been had the universe been differently made up. Nevertheless, if, as we may appropriately do, we judge of myth by the beliefs pervading it and the ideals supported and taught by it, we shall find that Chinese myth must be ranked among the best.

Myths and Legends

The general concepts thought about above, while they clarify the paucity of myth in China, clarify also the abundance of legend there. The six hundred years during which the Mongols, Mings, and Manchus sat upon the throne of China are barren of myth, but like all durations of the Chinese nationwide life are fertile in legend. And this chiefly for the reason that myths are more general, nationwide, magnificent, while legends are more regional, individual, human. And since, in China as in other places, the lower classes are as a guideline less educated and more superstitious than the upper classes-- have a certain amount of useful creativity, but insufficient to be self-critical-- legends, declined or perhaps ridiculed by the academic class when their knowledge has become sufficiently clinical, continue to be developed and believed in by the peasant and the occupant in districts far from the madding crowd long after myth, properly so called, has exhaled its last breath.

Cosmogony-p' an Ku and the Creation Myth
The Creator of deep space
The most obvious figure in Chinese cosmogony is P'an Ku. He it was who chiselled the universe out of Turmoil. According to Chinese ideas, he was the progeny of the original dual powers of Nature, the yin and the yang (to be considered presently), which, having in some incomprehensible way produced him, set him the task of giving form to Chaos and "making the heavens and the earth."

Some accounts describe him as the real creator of deep space--" the forefather of Paradise and earth and all that live and relocation and have their being." 'P'an' means 'the shell of an egg,' and 'Ku' 'to protect,' 'strong,' describing P'an Ku being hatched from out of Turmoil and to his settling the plan of the causes to which his beginning was due. The characters themselves might, though, mean nothing more than 'Investigates into antiquity,' though some bolder translators have designated to them the value if not the literal sense of 'aboriginal abyss,' or the Babylonian Tiamat, 'the Deep.'

P'an Ku is imagined as a man of dwarfish stature dressed in bearskin, or simply in leaves or with an apron of leaves. He has 2 horns on his head. In his right hand he holds a hammer and in his left a sculpt (in some cases these are reversed), the only executes he used in carrying out his great task. Other photos show him gone to in his labours by the 4 supernatural creatures-- the unicorn, phoenix, tortoise, and dragon; others again with the sun in one hand and the moon in the other, some of the firstfruits of his stupendous labours. (The reason for these being there will be apparent currently.) His job occupied eighteen 1,000 years, during which he formed the sun, moon, and stars, the heavens and the earth, himself increasing in stature day by day, being day-to-day six feet taller than the day before, until, his labours ended, he died that his works may live. His head ended up being the mountains, his breath the wind and clouds, his voice the thunder, his limbs the 4 quarters of the earth, his blood the rivers, his flesh the soil, his beard the constellations, his skin and hair the herbs and trees, his teeth, bones, and marrow the metals, rocks, and gemstones, his sweat the rain, and the insects sneaking over his body people, who hence had a lowlier origin even than the tears of Khepera in Egyptian cosmology.1.

This account of P'an Ku and his achievements is of Taoist origin. The Buddhists have given a somewhat different account of him, which is a late adjustment from the Taoist myth, and should not be misinterpreted for Buddhist cosmogony correct.2.

The Sun and the Moon.
In some of the images of P'an Ku he is represented, as already kept in mind, as holding the sun in one hand and the moon in the other. Sometimes they are in the form of those bodies, often in the classic character. The legend says that when P'an Ku put things in order in the lower world, he did not put these 2 stars in their correct courses, so they retired into the Han Sea, and the people dwelt in darkness. The Terrestrial Emperor sent out an officer, Terrestrial Time, with orders that they should come forth and take their spots in the heavens and give the world day and night. They refused to obey the order. They were reported to Ju Lai; P'an Ku was called, and, at the magnificent direction of Buddha, wrote the character for 'sun' in his left hand, and that for 'moon' in his right hand; and went to the Han Sea, and extended forth his left hand and called the sun, and then stretched forth his right-hand man and called the moon, at the exact same time repeating a charm fervently seven times; and they forthwith ascended on high, and apart time into day and night.3.

Other legends recount that P'an Ku had the head of a dragon and the body of a serpent; and that by breathing he triggered the wind, by opening his eyes he created day, his voice made the thunder, and so on.

Chapter 8: Several Myths

P'an Ku and Ymer.
Hence, we have the paradises and the earth fashioned by this terrific being in eighteen thousand years. With regard to him we may adapt the Scandinavian ballad:

It was Time's morning.
When P'an Ku lived;
There was no sand, no sea,
Nor cooling billows;

Earth there was none,
No lofty Heaven;
No area of living green;
Only a deep profound.

And it is fascinating to keep in mind, in passing, the similarity between this Chinese artificer of the universe and Ymer, the giant, who discharges the same functions in Scandinavian mythology. Though P'an Ku did not have the exact same type of birth nor meet the violent death of the latter, the results as concerns the beginning of deep space seem to have been pretty much the same.4.

P'an Ku a Late Creation.
But though the Chinese creation myth deals with primeval things it does not itself come from a primitive time. According to some authors whose views are entitled to respect, it was created during the 4th century A.D. by the Taoist recluse, Magistrate Ko Hung, author of the Shên hsien chuan (Bios of the Gods). The stunning person of P'an Ku is said to have been a concession to the well-known dislike of, or inability to understand, the abstract. He was conceived, some Chinese writers say, as the philosophical descriptions of the Universe were too recondite for the common mind to understand. That he did fulfil the purpose of providing the ordinary mind with a fairly quickly comprehensible picture of the creation might be confessed; but, as will presently be seen, it is over-stating the case to say that he was conceived with the set purpose of providing the regular mind with a concrete solution or illustration of the great problem. There is no proof that P'an Ku had existed as a tradition before the time when we meet the written account of him; and, what is more, there is no evidence that there existed any demand on the part of the well-known mind for any such solution or illustration. The normal mind would seem to have been either indifferent to or pleased with the abstruse cosmogonical and cosmological theories of the early sages for 1,000 years. The cosmogonies of the I ching, of Lao Tzǔ, Confucius (such as it was), Kuan Tzǔ, Mencius, Chuang Tzǔ, were impersonal. P'an Ku and his myth should be concerned rather as an accident than as a production arising from any abrupt flow of psychological forces or wind of discontent ruffling the placid Chinese mind. If the Chinese brought with them from Babylon or anywhere else the elements of a cosmogony, whether of a basically abstruse clinical nature or an individual mythological story, it must have

been subsequently forgotten or at least has not made it through in China. But for Ko Hung's eccentricity and his desire to experiment with cinnabar from Cochin-China to find the elixir of life, P'an Ku would probably never ever have been invented, and the Chinese mind would have been content to go on neglecting the issue or would have silently acquiesced in the abstract philosophical explanations of the learned which it did not comprehend. Chinese cosmogony would then have consisted specifically of the recondite impersonal metaphysics which the Chinese mind had captivated or been fed upon for the 9 hundred or more years preceding the development of the P'an Ku myth.

Nü Kua Shih, the Repairer of the Paradises.
It is very true that there exist a couple of other explanations of the origin of things which introduce a personal developer. There is, for instance, the legend-- very first discussed by Lieh Tzŭ (to whom we shall revert later)-- which represents Nü Kua Shih (also called Nü Wa and Nü Hsi), said to have been the sister and heir of Fu Hsi, the mythical sovereign whose reign is credited the years 2953-- 2838 B.C., as having been the developer of humans when the earth initially show upd from Turmoil. She (or he, for the sex appears uncertain), who had the "body of a snake and head of an ox" (or a human head and horns of an ox, according to some authors), "moulded yellow earth and made man." Ssŭ-ma Chêng, of the eighth century A.D., author of the Historical Records and of another work on the three great legendary emperors, Fu Hsi, Shên Nung, and Huang Ti, gives the following account of her: "Fu Hsi was followed by Nü Kua, who like him had the surname Fêng. Nü Kua had the body of a serpent and a human head, with the virtuous endowments of a divine sage. Towards the end of her reign there was among the feudatory princes Kung Kung, whose functions were the administration of penalty. Violent and enthusiastic, he ended up being a rebel, and looked for by the influence of water to get rid of that of wood [under which Nü Kua reigned] He did battle with Chu Jung [said to have been among the ministers of Huang Ti, and later the God of Fire], but was not triumphant; whereupon he struck his head against the Imperfect Mountain, Pu Chou Shan, and brought it down. The pillars of Heaven were broken and the corners of the earth gave way. Hereupon Nü Kua melted stones of the 5 colours to fix the heavens, and cut off the feet of the tortoise to set upright the 4 extremities of the earth.5 Collecting the ashes of reeds she stopped the flooding waters, and therefore saved the land of Chi, Chi Chou [the early seat of the Chinese sovereignty]".

Another account separates the name and makes Nü and Kua brother and sister, defining them as the only 2 people around. At the creation they were positioned at the foot of the K'un- lun Mountains. Then they prayed, saying, "If thou, O God, hast sent us to be man and marriage partner, the smoke of our sacrifice will stay in one place; but if not, it will be scattered." The smoke stayed fixed.

But though Nü Kua is said to have moulded the first man (or the first human entities) out of clay, it is to be noted that, being only the successor of Fu Hsi, long lines of rulers had preceded her of whom no account is given, and also that, as relates to the paradises and the earth at least, she is regarded as the repairer and not the developer of them.

Heaven-deaf (T'ien- lung) and Earth-dumb (Ti-ya), the two attendants of Wên Ch' ang, the God of Literature (see following chapter), have also been drawn into the cosmogonical net. From their union came the paradises and the earth, humanity, and all living things.

These and other brief and unelaborated personal cosmogonies, even if not to be considered spurious replicas, definitely have not become established in the Chinese mind as the clarification of the method which the vast universe became: in this sphere the P'an Ku legend reigns supreme; and, owing to its concrete, quickly apprehensible nature, has probably done so ever since the time of its innovation.

Early Cosmogony Dualistic
The duration before the appearance of the P'an Ku myth may be divided into 2 parts; that from some early unknown date up to about the middle of the Confucian epoch, say 500 B.C., and that from 500 B.C. to A.D. 400. We know that throughout the latter period the minds of Chinese academics were regularly occupied with speculations as to the origin of deep space. Before 500 B.C. we have no documentary remains telling us what the Chinese actually believed about the beginning of things; but it is exceedingly not likely that no theories or speculations at all concerning the beginning of themselves and their environments were formed by this intelligent people during the eighteen centuries or more which preceded the date at which we find the views held by them took into written form. It is safe to presume that the dualism which later occupied their philosophical thoughts to so great a degree as nearly to appear inseparable from them, and worked out so powerful an impact throughout the course of their history, was not only developing itself throughout that long period, but had gradually reached an advanced phase. We might even presume as to say that dualism, or its beginnings, existed in the very earliest times, for the belief in the 2nd self or ghost or double of the dead is in reality absolutely nothing else. And we find it operating with obviously undiminished energy after the Chinese mind had reached its maturity in the Sung dynasty.

The Canon of Changes
The Bible of Chinese dualism is the I ching, the Canon of Modifications (or Permutations). It is kept in great veneration both on account of its antiquity and also just because of the "unfathomable knowledge which is supposed to lie concealed under its mystical symbols." It is positioned initially in the list of the classics, or Holy Books, though it is not the oldest of them. When exactly the work itself on which the subsequent elaborations were founded was made up is not now understood. Its origin is credited to the legendary emperor Fu Hsi (2953-- 2838 B.C.). It does not furnish a cosmogony appropriate, but merely a dualistic system as a description, or attempted explanation, and even maybe only a record, of the constant changes (in contemporary philosophical language the "redistribution of matter and movement") going on everywhere. That clarification or record was used for purposes of divination. This dualistic system, by an easy addition, became a monism, and at the exact same time provided the Chinese with a cosmogony.

Chapter 9: The 5 Elements

The Five Aspects or Forces (wu hsing)-- which, according to the Chinese, are metal, air, fire, water, and wood-- are first discussed in Chinese literature in a chapter of the traditional Book of History.6 They play a very fundamental part in Chinese thought: 'aspects' meaning usually not so much the real compounds as the forces vital to human, life. They have to be seen in passing, because they were associated with the development of the cosmogonical ideas which happened in the eleventh and twelfth centuries A.D.

Monism

As their creativity grew, it was natural that the Chinese should start to ask themselves what, if the yang and the yin by their permutations produced, or gave shape to, all things, was it that produced the yang and the yin. When we see traces of this curious tendency we find ourselves on the borderland of dualism where the transition is happening into the realm of monism. However though there may have been a propensity towards monism in early times, it was only in the Sung dynasty that the philosophers definitely put behind the yang and the yin a Very first Cause-- the Grand Origin, Grand Extreme, Grand Terminus, or Ultimate Ground of Presence.7 They gave to it the name t' ai chi, and represented it by a concrete indication, the symbol of a circle. The complete plan shows the development of the Sixty-four Diagrams (kua) from the t' ai chi through the yang and the yin, the 4, Eight, Sixteen, and Thirty-two Diagrams successively. This conception was the work of the Sung thinker Chou Tun-i (A.D. 1017-- 73), frequently referred to as Chou Tzŭ, and his disciple Chu Hsi (A.D. 1130-- 1200), referred to as Chu Tzŭ or Chu Fu Tzŭ, the popular historian and Confucian analyst-- 2 of the best names in Chinese philosophy. It was at this time that the tide of positive imagination in China, tinged though it always was with classical Confucianism, arose to its greatest height. There is the thinker's seeking for causes. Yet in this matter of the First Cause we identify, in the full flood of Confucianism, the powerful influence of Taoist and Buddhist speculations. It has even been said that the Sung viewpoint, which grew, not from the I ching itself, but from the appendixes to it, is more Taoistic than Confucian. As it was with the P'an Ku legend, so was it with this more philosophical cosmogony. The more fertile Taoist and Buddhist imaginations caused the conservation of what the Confucianists, wondering about the wonderful, would have allowed to die a natural death. It was, after all, the magical foreign aspects which gave indicate-- we may appropriately say settled-- the early dualism by transforming it into monism, carrying philosophical speculation from the Knowable to the Unknowable, and providing the Chinese with their very first scientific theory of the beginning, not of the changes going on in deep space (on which they had already formed their opinions), but of the universe itself.

Chou Tzŭ's "T'ai Chi T' u".

Chou Tun-i, properly apotheosized as 'Prince in the Empire of Reason,' finished and integrated the philosophical world-conception which had hitherto obtained in the Chinese mind. He did not ask his fellow-countrymen to discard any part of what they had long held in high esteem: he raised the old theories from the sphere of science to that of approach by unifying them and bringing them to a focus. And he made this marriage intelligible to the Chinese mind by his well-known T'ai chi t' u, or Diagram of the Great Origin (or Grand Terminus), demonstrating that the Grand Original Cause, itself uncaused, produces the yang and the yin, these the 5 Elements, and so on, through the male and female norms (tao), to the production of all things.

Chu Hsi's Monistic Approach
The works of Chu Hsi, specifically his treatise on The Immaterial Principle [li] and Main Matter [ch' i], leave no doubt regarding the monism of his approach. In this work occurs the passage: "In deep space there exists no main matter lacking the immaterial principle; and no immaterial principle apart from primary matter"; and though the 2 are never ever split up "the immaterial principle [as Chou Tzŭ clarifies] is what is previous to form, while primary matter is what is subsequent to form," the idea being that the two are different symptoms of the same mysterious force from which all things continue.

It is unneeded to follow this philosophy along all the different branches which outgrew it, for we are here concerned only with the seed. We have observed how Chinese dualism ended up being a monism, and how while the monism was established the dualism was retained. It is this mono-dualistic theory, integrating the older and more recent approach, which in China, then as now, makes up the accepted explanation of the origin of things, of deep space itself and all that it consists of.

Lao Tzŭ's "Tao".
There are other cosmogonies in Chinese approach, but they need not apprehend us long. Lao Tzŭ (sixth century B.C.), in his Tao-tê ching, The Canon of Reason and Virtue (in the beginning entitled just Lao Tzŭ), offered to the then existing spread sporadic conceptions of the universe a literary form. His tao, or 'Way,' is the producer of Heaven and earth, it is "the mother of all things." His Way, which was "in the past God," is but a metaphorical expression for the manner in which things came at first into running out the primal nothingness, and how the phenomena of nature continue to go on, "in stillness and tranquility, without striving or sobbing." Lao Tzŭ is hence so far monistic, but he is also mystical, transcendental, even pantheistic. The way that can be walked is not the Immortal Way; the name that can be called is not the Immortal Name. The Unnameable is the originator of Heaven and earth; manifesting itself as the Nameable, it is "the mom of all things." "In Immortal Non-Being I see the Spirituality of Things; in Immortal Being their constraint. Though different under these 2 elements, they are the same in beginning; it is when development occurs that different names have to be used. It is while they are in the condition of sameness that the secret concerning them exists. This secret is certainly the secret of secrets. It is the door of all spirituality."

This tao, indefinable and in its essence unknowable, is "the fountain-head of all entities, and the norm of all actions. But it is not only the developmental principle of the universe; it also appears to be primordial matter: chaotic in its structure, born right before Paradise and earth, soundless, formless, standing alone in its privacy, and not changing, universal in its activity, and unrelaxing, without being exhausted, it is capable of ending up being the mother of the universe." And there we might leave it. There is no scheme of creation, correctly so called. The Unwalkable Way leads us to absolutely nothing farther in the way of a cosmogony.

Confucius's Agnosticism.
Confucius (551-- 479 B.C.) did not throw any light on the problem of origin. He did not speculate on the creation of things nor the end of them. He was not bothered to represent the origin of man, nor did he seek to know about his hereafter. He meddled neither with physics nor metaphysics. There might, he thought, be something on the other side of life, for he confessed the existence of spiritual entities. They had an influence on the living, as they triggered them to clothe themselves in ceremonious dress and take care of the sacrificial events. But we should not trouble ourselves about them, anymore than about supernatural things, or physical prowess, or monstrosities. How can we serve souls while we do not know how to serve guys? We feel the existence of something invisible and mysterious, but its nature and meaning are unfathomable for the human understanding to understand. The safest, certainly the only reasonable, course is that of the agnostic-- to leave alone the unknowable, while acknowledging its existence and its secret, and to try to comprehend knowable phenomena and guide our actions appropriately.

Between the monism of Lao Tzŭ and the positivism of Confucius on the one hand, and the landmark of the Taoistic transcendentalism of Chuang Tzŭ (4th and 3rd centuries B.C.) on the other, we find several "guesses at the riddle of existence" which need to be quickly kept in mind as links in the chain of Chinese speculative thought on this essential topic.

Mo Tzŭ and Creation
In the philosophy of Mo Ti (5th and 4th centuries B.C.), generally called Mo Tzŭ or Mu Tzŭ, the theorist of humanism and utilitarianism, we find the idea of creation. It was, he says, Paradise (which was anthropomorphically related to by him as an individual Supreme Being) who "created the sun, moon, and innumerable stars." His system closely looks like Christianity, but the great power of Confucianism as a weapon wielded against all challengers by its doughty defender Mencius (372-- 289 B.C.) is shown by the complete suppression of the impact of Mo Tzŭism at his hands. He even went so far regarding define Mo Tzŭ and those who thought with him as "wild animals."

Mencius and the First Cause
Mencius himself regarded Heaven as the First Cause, or Cause of Causes, but it was not the same personal Paradise as that of Mo Tzŭ. Nor does he hang any cosmogony upon it. His chief concern was to eulogize the doctrines of the great Confucius, and like him he preferred to let the beginning of the universe take care of itself.

Lieh Tzŭ's Absolute
Lieh Tzŭ (said to have lived in the 5th century B.C.), one of the brightest stars in the Taoist constellation, considered this nameable world as having developed from an unnameable outright being. The development did not happen through the direction of an individual will working out a strategy of creation: "In the beginning there was Turmoil [hun tun] It was a mingled potentiality of Form [hsing], Pneuma [ch'i], and Substance [chih] An Excellent Change [t'ai i] took place in it, and there was a Fantastic Starting [t'ai ch'u] which is the beginning of

Form. The Great Beginning developed a Fantastic Beginning [t'ai shih], which is the beginning of Pneuma. The Great Beginning was followed by the Great Blank [t'ai su], which is the very first development of Substance. Substance, Pneuma, and Form being all developed out of the primitive chaotic mass, this material world as it lies right before us came into existence." And that made it possible for Mayhem to progress was the Solitary Indeterminate (i tu or the tao), which is not created, but is able to produce everlastingly. And being both Singular and Indeterminate it tells us absolutely nothing determinate about itself.

Chuang Tzǔ's Super-tao

Chuang Chou (4th and third centuries B.C.), typically known as Chuang Tzǔ, the most dazzling Taoist of all, maintained with Lao Tzǔ that deep space started from the Anonymous, but it was if possible a more outright and transcendental Anonymous than that of Lao Tzǔ. He dwells on the relativity of knowledge; as when asleep he did not know that he was a guy dreaming that he was a butterfly, so when awake he did not know that he was not a butterfly dreaming that he was a guy.8 However "all is embraced in the eliminating unity of the tao, and the sensible man, entering the world of the Infinite, finds rest therein." And this tao, of which we hear so much in Chinese approach, was right before the Great Ultimate or Grand Terminus (t' ai chi), and "from it came the strange existence of God [ti] It produced Paradise, it produced earth."

Popular Cosmogony still Individual or Dualistic

These and other cosmogonies which the Chinese have devised, though it is required to note their presence to give a just idea of their cosmological speculations, need not, as I said, apprehend us long; and the reason why they need not do so is that, in the matter of cosmogony, the P'an Ku legend and the yin-yang system with its monistic elaboration occupy practically the whole field of the Chinese psychological vision. It is these 2-- the well-known and the clinical-- that we mean when we mention Chinese cosmogony. Though occasionally a stern sectarian might deny that deep space came from one or the other of these two ways, still, the general rule holds great. And I have handled them in this order since, though the P'an Ku legend belongs to the 4th century A.D., the I ching dualism was not, appropriately speaking, a cosmogony till Chou Tun-i made it one by the publication of his T'ai chi t'u in the lth century A.D. Over the unscientific and the clinical minds of the Chinese these two are critical.

Using the general principles specified in the preceding chapter, we find the same cause which operated to limit the development of folklore in general in China ran also in like way in this specific branch of it. With one exception Chinese cosmogony is non-mythological. The cautious and studiously accurate historians (whose work focused on being ex veritate, 'made of truth'), the sober literature, the huge influence of agnostic, matter-of-fact Confucianism, supported by the heavy Mencian weapons, are unassailable indications of a useful creativity which grew too quickly and became too rapidly scientific to admit of much skyrocketing into the worlds of fantasy. Unaroused by any strong stimulus in their ponderings over the riddle of the universe, the sober, plodding researchers and the calm, truth-loving theorists gained a serene victory over the mythologists.

Chapter 10: More about the Gods of China

The Birth of the Soul

The dualism noted in the last chapter is well highlighted by the Chinese temple. Whether as the outcome of the co-operation of the yin and the yang or of the final dissolution of P'an Ku, people originated. To the primitive mind the body and its shadow, an object and its reflection in water, reality and dream life, sensibility and insensibility (as in fainting, etc.), suggest the idea of another life parallel with this life and of the behaviors of the 'other self' in it. This 'other self,' this spirit, which leaves the body for longer or shorter intervals in dreams, swoons, death, might return or be brought back, and the body restore. Spirits which do not return or are not brought back might cause mischief, either alone, or by entry into another human or animal body and even an inanimate item, and should therefore be propitiated. For this reason worship and deification.

The Populous Otherworld

The Chinese pantheon has slowly ended up being so countless that there is scarcely a being or thing which is not, or has not been at some time or other, propitiated or worshipped. As there are great and evil people in this world, so there are gods and demons in the Otherworld: we find a polytheism restricted only by a polydemonism. The dualistic hierarchy is almost all-embracing. To get a clear idea of the populated Otherworld, of the supernal and infernal hosts and their companies, it needs but to imagine the social structure in its highlights as it existed throughout the majority of Chinese history, and to make sure additions. The social structure consisted of the ruler, his court, his civil, army, and ecclesiastical authorities, and his subjects (classified as Scholars-- authorities and gentry-- Agriculturists, Artisans, and Merchants, in that order).

Praise of Shang Ti

When these passed away, their other selves continued to exist and to hold the same rank in the spirit world as they did in this one. The ti, emperor, ended up being the Shang Ti, Emperor on High, who stay in T'ien, Heaven (initially the great dome).1 And Shang Ti, the Emperor on High, was worshipped by ti, the emperor here below, so as to pacify or please him-- to ensure a continuation of his benevolence on his behalf in the world of spirits. Confusion of ideas and paucity of primitive language result in personification and praise of a thing or being in which a spirit has used up its house in place of or in addition to praise of the spirit itself. Thus Heaven (T'ien) itself came to be personified and worshipped in addition to Shang Ti, the Emperor who had gone to Paradise, and who was considered as the chief ruler in the spiritual world. The worship of Shang Ti was in existence before that of T'ien was introduced. Shang Ti was worshipped by the emperor and his family as their forefather, or the head of the hierarchy of their forefathers. Individuals could not praise Shang Ti, for to do so would indicate a familiarity or a claim of relationship punishable with death. The emperor worshipped his ancestors, the authorities theirs, the people theirs. But, in the exact same way and sense that the people worshipped the emperor in the world, as the 'father' of the nation, namely, by love and obeisance, so also could they in this way and this sense worship Shang Ti. An Englishman may take off his hat as the king passes in the street to his coronation without taking any part in the main service in Westminster Abbey. So the 'praise' of Shang Ti by the people was not done officially or with any unique ritualistic or on repaired State occasions, as when it comes to the worship of Shang Ti by the emperor. This, subject to a credentials to be mentioned later, is actually all that is meant (or should be meant) when it is said that the Chinese worship Shang Ti.

As relates to sacrifices to Shang Ti, these could be offered officially only by the emperor, as High Priest in the world, who was attended or helped in the ceremonies by members of his own family or clan or the appropriate State authorities (often, even in relatively modern times, members of the imperial family or clan). In these main sacrifices, which formed part of the State worship, the people could not take part; nor did they at first offer sacrifices to Shang Ti in their own homes or elsewhere. In what way and to what extent they did so later will be revealed presently.

Worship of T'ien
Owing to T'ien, Paradise, the residence of the spirits, ending up being personified, it became worshipped not only by the emperor, but by the people also. But there was a big difference between these 2 worships, because the emperor performed his praise of Paradise formally at the great altar of the Temple of Heaven at Peking (in early times at the altar in the suburban area of the capital), whereas the people (continuing always to worship their ancestors) worshipped Heaven, when they did so at all-- the tradition being observed by some and not by others, just as in Western nations some people go to church, while other people stay away-- generally at the time of the New Year, in a basic, unceremonious way, by lighting some incense-sticks and waving them towards the sky in the courtyards of their own houses or in the street just outside their doors.

Confusion of Shang Ti and T'ien
The credentials necessary to the above description is that, as time went on and especially since the Sung dynasty (A.D. 960-- 1280), much confusion emerged relating to Shang Ti and T'ien, and thus it happened that the terms ended up being blended and their definitions obscure. This confusion of ideas has prevailed down to the present time. One outcome of this is that the people might often state, when they wave their incense-sticks or light their candles, that their humble sacrifice is made to Shang Ti, whom in reality they have no right either to praise or to use sacrifice to, but whom they may unofficially pay respect and make obeisance to, as they might and did to the emperor behind the high boards on the roadsides which shielded him from their view as he was borne along in his sophisticated procession on the few events when he came forth from the royal city.

Hence we find that, while only the emperor could praise and sacrifice to Shang Ti, and only he could formally worship and sacrifice to T'ien, the people who early personified and worshipped T'ien, as already revealed, came, owing to confusion of the significances of Shang Ti and T'ien, unofficially to 'worship' both, but only in the sense and to the level showed, and to use 'sacrifices' to both, also only in the sense and to the level showed. However for these credentials, the declaration that the Chinese worship and sacrifice to Shang Ti and T'ien would be apt to communicate an incorrect idea.

From this it will appear that Shang Ti, the Supreme Ruler on High, and T'ien, Heaven (later personified), do not mean 'God' in the sense that the word is used in the Christian religion. To state that they do, as so many writers on China have done, without explaining the necessary distinctions, is misguiding. That Chinese religious belief was or is "a monotheistic worship of God" is more disproved by the simple fact that Shang Ti and T'ien do not appear in the list of the popular pantheon at all, though all the other gods are there represented. Neither Shang Ti nor T'ien mean the God of Abraham, Isaac, and Jacob, or the Dad, Son, and Holy Ghost of the New Testament. Did they mean this, the efforts of the Christian missionaries to convert the Chinese would be mostly superfluous. The Christian faith, even the Holy Trinity, is a monotheism. That the Chinese religion (although a summary of extracts from the majority of foreign books on China may point to its being so) is not a monotheism, but a polytheism and even a pantheism (as long as that term is taken in the sense of universal deification and not in that of one spiritual being immanent in all things), the rest of the chapter will abundantly prove.

There have been 3 periods in which gods have been created in abnormally large numbers: that of the legendary emperor Hsien Yüan (2698-- 2598 B.C.), that of Chiang Tzŭ-ya (in the twelfth century B.C.), and that of the very first emperor of the Ming dynasty (in the fourteenth century A.D.).

The Otherworld Similar to this World
The similarity of the Otherworld to this world above alluded to is well revealed by Du Bose in his Dragon, Image, and, Satanic force, from which I estimate the following passages:

" The world of spirits is a specific equivalent of the Chinese Empire, or, as has been mentioned, it is 'China tilled under'; this is the world of light; put out the lights and you have Tartarus. China has eighteen [now twenty-two] provinces, so has Hades; each province has 8 or 9 prefects, or departments; so each province in Hades has 8 or nine departments; every prefect or department averages ten counties, so every department in Hades has 10 counties. In Soochow the Ruler, the provincial Treasurer, the Criminal Judge, the Intendant of Circuit, the Prefect or Departmental Ruler, and the three District Magistrates or County Governors each have temples with their apotheoses in the other world. Not only these, but every yamên secretary, runner, executioner, policeman, and constable has his counterpart in the land of darkness. The market-towns have also mandarins of lower rank in charge, besides a host of revenue collectors, the bureau of federal government works and other departments, with some hundred 1000 officials, who all rank as gods beyond the grave. These divine entities are citizens; the military having a comparable gradation for the armies of Hades, whose captains are gods, and whose battalions are fiends.

" The of this wonderful scheme for the spirits of the dead, having no higher standard, moved to the authorities of that world the etiquette, tastes, and venality of their correlate authorities in the Chinese Federal government, therefore making it needed to use similar ways to appease the one which are found essential to move the other. All the State gods have their assistants, attendants, door-keepers, runners, horses, horsemen, investigators, and executioners, corresponding in every specific to those of Chinese authorities of the same rank." (Pp. 358--359.)

This likeness clarifies also why the hierarchy of entities in the Otherworld concerns itself not only with the affairs of the Otherworld, but with those of this world too. So faithful is the similarity that we find the gods (the term is used in this chapter to consist of goddesses, who are, however, reasonably couple of) subjected to tons of the guidelines and conditions existing on this earth. Not only do they, as already revealed, vary in rank, but they hold levées and audiences and might be promoted for recognized services, just as the Chinese authorities are. They "may arise from a modest position to one near the Pearly Emperor, who provides the reward of merit for ruling well the affairs of guys. The correlative divine entities of the mandarins are only of equivalent rank, yet the fact that they have been apotheosized makes them their superiors and in shape things of worship. Chinese mandarins turn in office, usually every 3 years, and then there is a corresponding change in Hades. The image in the temple remains the same, but the spirit which stays in the clay tabernacle changes, so the idol has a different name, birthday, and tenant. The priests are notified by the Great Wizard of the Dragon Tiger Mountain, but how can the people know gods which are not the same to-day as the other day?"

The gods also enjoy amusements, wed, sin, are punished, die, are resurrected, or die and are changed, or die finally.

The Three Religious beliefs
We have in China the universal praise of ancestors, which constitutes (or did till A.D. 1912) the State religion, typically referred to as Confucianism, and in addition we have the gods of the specific faiths (which also originally took their arise in ancestor-worship), specifically, Buddhism and Taoism. (Other faiths, though endured, are not acknowledged as Chinese faiths.) It is with a short account of this great hierarchy and its folklore that we will now concern ourselves.

Besides the regular ancestor-worship (as distinct from the State praise) the people required to Buddhism and Taoism, which became the well-known religions, and the literati also honoured the gods of these 2 sects. Buddhist deities gradually became installed in Taoist temples, and the Taoist immortals were given seats next to the Buddhas in their sanctuaries. Every one bought from the god who appeared to him the most popular and the most financially rewarding. There even happened unified in the exact same temple and worshipped at the exact same altar the 3 religious creators or figure-heads, Confucius, Buddha, and Lao Tzŭ. The 3 religious beliefs were even considered forming one whole, or at least, though different, as having one and the same object: san êrh i yeh, or han san wei i, "the three are one," or "the 3 join to form one" (a quotation from the phrase T'ai chi han san wei i of Fang Yü-lu: "When they reach the severe the 3 are seen to be one"). In the well-known pictorial depictions of the temple this impartiality is plainly revealed.

The Super-triad

The toleration, fraternity, or co-mixture of the three religions-- ancestor-worship or Confucianism, Chinese Buddhism, and Taoism-- clarifies the substance nature of the triune head of the Chinese pantheon. The numerous deities of Buddhism and Taoism culminate each in a triad of gods (the 3 Precious Ones and the 3 Pure Ones respectively), but the three religions collectively have also a triad compounded of one representative member of each. This general or super-triad is, naturally, made up of Confucius, Lao Tzǔ, and Buddha. This is the officially decreed order, though it is varied occasionally by Buddha being put in the centre (the spot of honour) as an act of ritualistic deference revealed to a 'stranger' or 'guest' from another nation.

Praise of the Living

Right before continuing to think about the gods of China in detail, it is required to note that ancestor-worship, which, as right before specified, is worship of the ghosts of departed persons, who are generally but not inevitably loved ones of the worshipper, has at times a sort of preliminary phase in this world including the worship of living beings. Emperors, viceroys, popular officials, or people cherished for their kind deeds have had altars, temples, and images put up to them, where they are worshipped in the exact same way as those who have already "shuffled off this mortal coil." The most usual cases are maybe those of the worship of living emperors and those in which some high authority who has acquired the gratitude of the people is transferred to another post. The clarification is basic. The 2nd self which exists after death is identical with the second self inhabiting the body throughout life. Therefore it might be propitiated or gratified by sacrifices of food, drink, and so on, or theatricals performed in its honour, and continue its security and good offices even though now far away.

Confucianism

Confucianism (Ju Chiao) is said to be the religious belief of the learned, and the learned were the authorities and the literati or lettered class, which includes academics waiting on posts, those who have couldn't get posts (or, though certified, prefer to live in retirement), and those who have retired from posts. Of this 'religious belief' it has been said:

" The name embraces education, letters, principles, and political viewpoint. Its head was not a religious man, practised couple of spiritual rites, and taught nothing about faith. In its usual acceptation the term Confucianist means 'a gentleman and a academic'; he might praise only once a year, yet he comes from the Church. Unlike its two sisters, it has no priesthood, and fundamentally is not a religion at all; yet with the many rites implanted on the original tree it becomes a religious beliefs, and the one most difficult to handle. Thought about as a Church, the classics are its scriptures, the schools its churches, the teachers its priests, ethics its faith, and the written character, so sacred, its symbol." 3.

Confucius not a God.

It should be noted that Confucius himself is not a god, though he has been and is worshipped (66,000 animals used to be offered to him every year; probably the number is about the same now). Suggestions have been made to make him the God of China and Confucianism the religious belief of China, so that he and his faith would hold the exact same relative positions that Christ and Christianity do in the West. I was present at the prolonged dispute which occurred on this subject in the Chinese Parliament in February 1917, but in spite of tons of long, learned, and significant speeches, primarily by academics of the old school, the movement was not brought. However, the praise accorded to Confucius was and is (other than by 'brand-new' or 'young' China) of so extreme a nature that he might practically be described as the great unapotheosized god of China.4 Some of his portraits even credit him superhuman characteristics. However in spite of all this the simple fact remains that Confucius has not been appointed a god and holds no exequatur entitling him to that rank.

If we explore the reason of this we find that, impressive though it may seem, Confucius is classed by the Chinese not as a god (shên), but as a devil (kuei). A brief historic declaration will make the matter clear.

In the classical Li chi, Book of Ritualistic, we find the categorical task of the worship of certain challenge certain subjective beings: the emperor worshipped Heaven and earth, the feudal princes the mountains and rivers, the officials the hearth, and the literati their ancestors. Heaven, earth, mountains, rivers, and hearth were called shên (gods), and ancestors kuei (demons). This difference is due to Paradise being considered as the god and the people as satanic forces-- the upper is the god, the lower the fiend or devil. Though kuei were generally bad, the term in Chinese consists of both good and evil spirits. In old times those who had by their meritorious virtue while in the world prevented calamities from the people were posthumously worshipped and called gods, but those who were worshipped by their descendants only were called spirits or devils.

In the praise of Confucius by emperors of different dynasties (details of which need not be given here) the greatest titles gave on him were Hsien Shêng, 'Former or Ancestral Saint,' and even Win Hsüan Wang, 'Accomplished and Renowned Prince,' and other ones containing like epithets. When for his image or idol there was (in the eleventh year-- A.D. 1307-- of the reign-period Ta Tê of the Emperor Ch' êng Tsung of the Yüan dynasty) replaced the tablet now seen in the Confucian temples, these were the engravings inscribed on it. In the inscriptions authoritatively put on the tablets the word shên does not take place; in those cases where it does occur it has been placed there (as by the Taoists) unlawfully and without authority by too ardent devotees. Confucius might not be called a shên, since there is no record demonstrating that the great ethical teacher was ever apotheosized, or that any order was considered that the character shên was to be applied to him.

The God of Literature

In addition to the ancestors of whose praise it truly consists, Confucianism has in its temple the specialized gods worshipped by the literati. Naturally the chief of these is Wên Ch' ang, the God of Literature. The account of him (which differs in several particulars in different Chinese works) relates that he was a man of the name of Chang Ya, who was born throughout the T'ang dynasty in the kingdom of Yüeh (modern Chêkiang), and went to live at Tzŭ T'ung in Ssŭch' uan, where his intelligence raised him to the position of President of the Board of Ceremonies. Another account refers to him as Chang Ya Tzŭ, the Soul or Spirit of Tzŭ T'ung, and mentions that he held office in the Chin dynasty (A.D. 265-- 316), and was killed in a battle. Another again specifies that under the Sung dynasty (A.D. 960-- 1280), in the 3rd year (A.D. 1000) of the reign-period Hsien P'ing of the Emperor Chên Tsung, he repressed the revolt of Wang Chün at Ch' êng Tu in Ssǔch' uan. General Lei Yu-chung triggered to be shot into the besieged town arrows to which notices were attached welcoming the inhabitants to give up. All of a sudden a man installed a ladder, and indicating the rebels cried in a loud voice: "The Spirit of Tzǔ T'ung has sent me to inform you that the town will fall into the hands of the enemy on the twentieth day of the ninth moon, and not a bachelor will get away death." Efforts to strike down this prophet of evil failed, for he had already disappeared. The town was caught on the day suggested. The general, as a reward, caused the temple of Tzǔ T'ung's Spirit to be repaired, and sacrifices offered to it.

The thing of worship nowadays in the temples committed to Wên Ch' ang is Tzǔ T'ung Ti Chün, the God of Tzǔ T'ung. The practical flexibility of dualism allowed Chang to have as many as seventeen reincarnations, which varied over a period of some 3 thousand years.

Different emperors at various times bestowed upon Wên Ch' ang honorific titles, until eventually, in the Yüan, or Mongol, dynasty, in the reign Yen Yu, in A.D. 1314, the title was conferred on him of Supporter of the Yüan Dynasty, Diffuser of Renovating Influences, Ssǔ-lu of Wên Ch' ang, God and Lord. He was therefore apotheosized, and took his spot among the gods of China. By steps couple of or tons of a man in China has typically become a god.

Wên Ch' ang and the Great Bear
Thus we have the God of Literature, Wên Ch' ang Ti Chün, duly set up in the Chinese temple, and sacrifices were offered to him in the schools.

But scholars, specifically those ready to go into for the general public competitive examinations, worshipped as the God of Literature, or as his palace or home (Wên Ch'ang), the star K'uei in the Great Bear, or Dipper, or Bushel-- the latter name stemmed from its resemblance in shape to the measure used by the Chinese and called tou. The term K'uei was more generally applied to the four stars forming the body or square part of the Dipper, the 3 forming the tail or handle being called Shao or Piao. How all this happened is another story.

An expert, as popular for his literary ability as his facial deformities, had been admitted as first academician at the cosmopolitan examinations. It was the habit that the Emperor should give with his own hand a rose of gold to the fortunate prospect. This academic, whose name was Chung K'uei, presented himself according to custom to get the benefit which by right was because of him. At the sight of his repulsive face the Emperor refused the golden rose. In despair the unhappy turned down one went and tossed himself into the sea. At the moment when he was being choked by the waters a mystical fish or monster called ao raised him on its back and brought him to the surface area. K'uei rose to Paradise and became arbiter of the destinies of men of letters. His house was said to be the star K'uei, a name given by the Chinese to the sixteen stars of the constellation or 'estate' of Andromeda and Pisces. The academics quite quickly began to praise K'uei as the God of Literature, and to represent it on a column in the temples. Then sacrifices were offered to it. This star or constellation was considered the palace of the god. The legend generated an expression frequently used in Chinese of one who comes out initially in an evaluation, particularly, tu chan ao t'ou, "to stand alone on the sea-monster's head." It is especially to be kept in mind that though the two K'ueis have the same noise they are represented by different characters, and that the two constellations are not the exact same, but are situated in widely different parts of the heavens.

How then did it happen that experts worshipped the K'uei in the Great Bear as the house of the God of Literature? (It may be said in passing that a literary people could not have chosen a more appropriate palace for this god, since the Great Bear, the 'Chariot of Paradise,' is considered as the centre and governor of the whole universe.) The worship, we saw, was at initially that of the star K'uei, the apotheosized 'homely,' successful, but rejected prospect. As time went on, there was a general demand for a practical, concrete representation of the star-god: a simple character did not please the well-known taste. But it was no simple matter to comply with the need. Ultimately, directed doubtless by the community of pronunciation, they substituted for the star or group of stars K'uei ,5 venerated in old times, a new star or group of stars K'uei , forming the square part of the Bushel, Dipper, or Great Bear. But for this again no bodily image could be found, so the form of the written character itself was taken, and so drawn as to represent a kuei (3) (disembodied spirit, or ghost) with its foot raised, and bearing aloft a tou (4) (bushel-measure). The love was hence lost, for the constellation K'uei (2) was mistaken for K'uei , the correct thing of praise. It was because of this confusion by the academics that the Northern Bushel became worshipped as the God of Literature.

Wên Ch' ang and Tzǔ T'ung
This worship had nothing whatever to do with the Spirit of Tzǔ T'ung, but the Taoists have connected Chang Ya with the constellation in another way by saying that Shang Ti, the Supreme Ruler, turned over Chang Ya's child with the management of the palace of Wên Ch' ang. And experts gradually got the habit of saying that they owed their success to the Spirit of Tzǔ T'ung, which they falsely represented as being an incarnation of the star Wên Ch' ang. This is how Chang Ya came to have the honorific title of Wên Ch' ang, but, as a Chinese author mentions, Chang belonged correctly to Ssǔch' uan, and his worship must be restricted to that province. The literati there venerated him as their master, and as a mark of affection and thankfulness built a temple to him; but in doing so they had no objective of making him the God of Literature. "There being no real connexion between Chang Ya and K'uei, the praise ought to be stopped." The gadget of integrating the personality of the client of literature enthroned among the stars with that of the deified mortal canonized as the Spirit of Tzǔ T'ung was basically a Taoist technique. "The thaumaturgic track record assigned to the Spirit of Chang Ya Tzǔ was confined for centuries to the valleys of Ssǔch' uan, until at some duration antecedent to the reign Yen Yu, in A.D. 1314, a combination was arranged between the functions of the local god and those of the stellar customer of literature. Imperial sanction was acquired for this stroke of priestly shrewd; and notwithstanding demonstrations constantly repeated by orthodox sticklers for precision in the religious canon, the composite divine being has kept his claims undamaged, and an inseparable connexion between the God of Literature created by imperial patent and the spirit lodged amongst the stars of Ursa Major is completely acknowledged in the State

ritualistic of the present day." A temple committed to this divinity by the State exists in every city of China, besides other ones put up as personal benefactions or speculations.

Wherever Wên Ch' ang is worshipped there will also be found a different depiction of K'uei Hsing, showing that while the main deity has been enabled to 'obtain magnificence' from the well-known god, and even to assume his personality, the independent existence of the outstanding spirit is nevertheless sedulously preserved. The spot of the latter in the heavens above is usually represented by the lodgment of his idol in an upper floor or tower, known as the K'uei Hsing Ko or K'uei Hsing Lou. Here students worship the customer of their occupation with incense and prayers. Therefore, the old outstanding divinity still largely monopolizes the popular idea of a defender of literature and research study, notwithstanding that the deified recluse of Tzŭ T'ung has been included this capability to the State pantheon for more than five hundred years.

Heaven-deaf and Earth-dumb
The popular likenesss of Wên Ch' ang illustrate the god himself and 4 other figures. The main and biggest is the demure portrait of the god, clothed in blue and holding a sceptre in his left hand. Behind him stand two vibrant attendants. They are the servant and groom who always accompany him on his journeys (on which he rides a white horse). Their names are respectively Hsüan T'ung- tzŭ and Ti-mu, 'Sombre Youth' and 'Earth-mother'; more frequently they are called T'ien- lung, 'Deaf Celestial,' and Ti-ya, 'Mute Terrestrial,' or 'Deaf as Paradise' and 'Mute as Earth.' Therefore, they cannot reveal the secrets of their master's administration as he disperses intellectual gifts, literary ability, etc. Their cosmogonical connexion has already been referred to in a previous chapter.

Picture of K'uei Hsing
In front of Wên Ch' ang, on his left, stands K'uei Hsing. He is represented as of diminutive stature, with the visage of a demon, holding a writing-brush in his right-hand man and a tou in his left, one of his legs kicking up behind-- the figure being undoubtedly planned as an impersonation of the character k' uei .6 He is considered as the supplier of literary degrees, and was invoked above all in order to obtain success at the competitive evaluations. His images and temples are found in all towns. In the temples devoted to Wên Ch' ang there are always 2 secondary altars, one of which is consecrated to his praise.

Mr Redcoat
The other is devoted to Chu I, 'Mr Redcoat.' He and K'uei Hsing are represented as the two inseparable companions of the God of Literature. The legend related of Chu I is as follows:

During the T'ang dynasty, in the reign-period Chien Chung (A.D. 780-- 4) of the Emperor Tê Tsung, the Princess T'ai Yin saw that Lu Ch'i, a native of Hua Chou, had the bones of an Immortal, and wished to marry him.

Ma P' o, her neighbour, introduced him one day into the Crystal Palace for an interview with his future wife. The Princess gave him the choice of 3 careers: to live in the Dragon Prince's Palace, with the guarantee of immortal life, to enjoy immortality among the people on the earth, or to have the honour of becoming a minister of the Empire. Lu Ch' i first answered that he wishes to live in the Crystal Palace. The young lady, overjoyed, said to him: "I am Princess T'ai Yin. I will at once inform Shang Ti, the Supreme Ruler." A minute later the arrival of a celestial messenger was announced. Two officers bearing flags preceded him and conducted him to the foot of the flight of steps. He then presented himself as Chu I, the envoy of Shang Ti.

Addressing himself to Lu Ch' i, he asked: "Do you wish to reside in the Crystal Palace?" The latter did not reply. T'ai Yin advised him to give his answer, but he continued keeping silent. The Princess in despair retired to her apartment or condo, and highlighted 5 pieces of valuable fabric, which she presented to the magnificent envoy, pleading him to have patience a little bit longer and wait for the answer. After a long time, Chu I repeated his question. Then Lu Ch' i in a firm voice answered: "I have consecrated my life to the tough labour of research study, and desire to attain to the self-respect of minister on this earth."

T'ai Yin ordered Ma P' o to perform Lu Ch' i from the palace. From that day his face ended up being transformed: he obtained the lips of a dragon, the head of a panther, the green face of an Immortal, and so on. He took his degree, and was promoted to be Director of the Censorate. The Emperor, valuing the common sense displayed in his advice, selected him a minister of the Empire.

From this legend it would appear that Chu I is the purveyor of main posts; however, in practice, he is more generally considered as the protector of weak candidates, as the God of Good Luck for those who present themselves at the examinations with a somewhat light equipment of literary knowledge. The unique legend associating with this rôle is understood all over in China. It is as follows:

Mr Redcoat nods his Head
An examiner, engaged in remedying the essays of the prospects, after a superficial examination of one of the essays, put it on one side as manifestly inferior, being quite determined not to pass the prospect who had composed it. The essay, moved by some mystical power, was changed in front of his eyes, as though to welcome him to analyze it more diligently. At the exact same time a reverend old man, dressed in a red garment, unexpectedly appeared before him, and by a nod of his head gave him to understand that he ought to pass the essay. The inspector, shocked at the novelty of the event, and strengthened by the approval of his transcendent visitor, admitted the author of the essay to the literary degree.

Chu I, like K'uei Hsing, is invoked by the literati as an effective protector and help to success. When anybody with but a poor chance of passing presents himself at an evaluation, his good friends motivate him by the well-known expression: "Who knows but that Mr Redcoat will nod his head?"

Mr Golden Cuirass

Chu I is sometimes joined by another personage, called Chin Chia, 'Mr Golden Cuirass.' Like K'uei Hsing and Chu I he has charge of the interests of experts, but varies from them in that he holds a flag, which he has only to wave in front of a home for the family inhabiting it to be ensured that among their descendants will be some who will win literary honours and be promoted to high offices under the State.

Though Chin Chia is the protector of experts, he is also the redoubtable avenger of their evil actions: his flag is saluted as a promise, but his sword is the horror of the wicked.

The God of War
Still another client divine being of literature is the God of War. "How," it may be asked, "can so peaceful a people as the Chinese put so tranquil a profession as literature under the patronage of so military a divine being as the God of War?" But that question betrays ignorance of the character of the Chinese Kuan Ti. He is not a harsh tyrant delighting in fight and the slaying of enemies: he is the god who can avert war and protect the people from its horrors.

A youth, whose name was initially Chang-shêng, later changed to Shou-chang, and then to Yün-chang, who was born near Chieh Liang, in Ho Tung (now the town of Chieh Chou in Shansi), and was of an intractable nature, having actually annoyed his father and mother, was shut up in a room from which he escaped by breaking through the window. In one of the neighbouring houses he heard a girl and an old man weeping and regretting. Going to the foot of the wall of the substance, he asked the reason of their sorrow. The old man replied that though his daughter was already engaged, the uncle of the regional authority, smitten by her charm, wished to make her his courtesan. His petitions to the authority had only been declined with curses.

Next to himself with rage, the youth took a sword and went and killed both the official and his uncle. He left through the T'ung Kuan, the pass to Shensi. Having with problem kept away from capture by the barrier officials, he knelt down at the side of a brook to clean his face; when lo! his appearance was entirely changed. His skin tone had ended up being reddish-grey, and he was absolutely unrecognizable. He then presented himself with guarantee before the officers, who asked him his name. "My name is Kuan," he replied. It was by that name that he was afterwards understood.

The Meat-seller's Obstacle
One day he got to Chu-chou, a reliant sub-prefecture of Peking, in Chihli. There Chang Fei, a butcher, who had been selling his meat all the early morning, at midday decreased what stayed into a well, positioned over the mouth of the well a stone weighing twenty-five pounds, and said with a sneer: "If anyone can raise that stone and take my meat, I will make him a present of it!" Kuan Yü, going up to the edge of the well, raised the stone with the exact same ease as he would a tile, took the meat, and left. Chang Fei pursued him, and ultimately the 2 came to blows, but no one dared to separate them. Just then Liu Pei, a hawker of straw shoes, showed up, interposed, and stopped the battle. The community of ideas which they found they possessed quickly triggered a firm friendship between the 3 guys.

The Oath in the Peach-orchard

Another account represents Liu Pei and Chang Fei as having gotten in a village inn to drink white wine, when a guy of massive stature pushing a wheelbarrow stopped at the door to rest. As he seated himself, he hailed the waiter, saying: "Bring me some wine rapidly, since I need to speed up to reach the town to get in the army."

Liu Pei looked at this man, nine feet in height, with a beard 2 feet long. His face was the colour of the fruit of the jujube-tree, and his lips carmine. Eyebrows like sleeping silkworms shaded his phoenix eyes, which were a scarlet red. Horrible undoubtedly was his bearing.

" What is your name?" asked Liu Pei. "My family name is Kuan, my own name is Yü, my surname Yün Chang," he responded. "I am from the Ho Tung country. For the last 5 or 6 years I have been roaming about the world as a fugitive, to get away from my chase afterrs, as I killed a powerful man of my country who was oppressing the poor people. I hear that they are gathering a body of soldiers to crush the brigands, and I should like to join the exploration."

Chang Fêi, also named Chang I Tê, is described as eight feet in height, with round shining eyes in a panther's head, and a pointed chin bristling with a tiger's beard. His voice looked like the rumbling of thunder. His ardour was just like that of a fiery steed. He hailed Cho Chün, where he had some fertile farms, and was a butcher and wine-merchant.

Liu Pei, surnamed Hsüan Tê, otherwise Hsien Chu, was the 3rd member of the group.

The 3 men went to Chang Fei's farm, and on the morrow met together in his peach-orchard, and sealed their friendship with an oath. Having actually procured a black ox and a white horse, with the numerous accessories to a sacrifice, they immolated the victims, burnt the incense of friendship, and after two times prostrating themselves took this oath:

" We 3, Liu Pei, Kuan Yû, and Chang Fei, already unified by mutual friendship, though coming from different clans, now bind ourselves by the union of our hearts, and join our forces in order to help one another in times of risk.

" We wish to pay to the State our financial obligation of faithful residents and give peace to our black-haired compatriots. We do not ask if we were born in the exact same year, the same month, or on the same day, but we desire only that the same year, the exact same month, and the same day may find us united in death. Might Paradise our King and Earth our Queen see clearly our hearts! If any among us violate justice or forget advantages, might Heaven and Man join to punish him!"

The oath having been officially taken, Liu Pei was saluted as senior brother, Kuan Yü as the 2nd, and Chang Fei as the youngest. Their sacrifice to Heaven and earth ended, they killed an ox and served a banquet, to which the soldiers of the district were welcomed to the number of 3 hundred or more. They all drank copiously till they were intoxicated. Liu Pei enrolled the peasants; Chang Fei obtained for them horses and arms; and then they set out to make war on the Yellow Turbans (Huang Chin Tsei). Kuan Yü showed himself worthy of the affection which Liu Pei revealed to him; brave and generous, he never ever turned aside from danger. His fidelity was revealed particularly on one occasion when, having actually been taken detainee by Ts' ao Ts' ao, together with 2 of Liu Pei's wives, and having actually been allocated a typical sleeping-apartment with his fellow-captives, he preserved the girls' reputation and his own credibility by standing all night at the door of the room with a lighted lantern in his hand.

Into details of the numerous exploits of the 3 Sibling of the Peach-orchard we really need not get in here. They are written in full in the book of the Story of the Three Kingdoms, a romance in which every Chinese who can read takes eager delight. Kuan Yü stayed faithful to his oath, despite the fact that lured with a marquisate by the great Ts' ao Ts' ao, but he was at length captured by Sun Ch' üan and put to death (A.D. 219). Long celebrated as the most popular of China's army heroes, he was ennobled in A.D. 1120 as Faithful and Loyal Duke. 8 years later he had given to him by letters patent the still more remarkable title of Splendid Prince and Pacificator. The Emperor Wên (A.D. 1330-- 3) of the Yüan dynasty added the appellation Warrior Prince and Civilizer, and, finally, the Emperor Wan Li of the Ming dynasty, in 1594, gave on him the title of Faithful and Loyal Great Ti, Advocate of Paradise and Protector of the Kingdom. He therefore ended up being a god, a ti, and has since received worship as Kuan Ti or Wu Ti, the God of War. Temples (1600 State temples and countless littler ones) set up in his honour are to be seen in all parts of the nation. He is just one of the most well-known gods of China Throughout the last half-century of the Manchu Period his fame greatly increased. In 1856 he is said to have appeared in the paradises and successfully turned the tide of fight in favour of the Imperialists. His portrait awaits every camping tent, but his worship is not confined to the officials and the army, for tons of trades and occupations have chosen him as a tutelary saint. The sword of the public executioner used to be kept within the precincts of his temple, and after an execution the administering magistrate would stop there to praise for worry the ghost of the criminal may follow him home. He knew that the spirit would not dare to enter Kuan Ti's presence.

Therefore, the Chinese have no less than three gods of literature-- maybe not too many for so literary a people. A fourth, a Taoist god, will be discussed later.

Buddhism and its mythology have formed a fundamental part of Chinese thought for almost 2 1000 years. The faith was given China about A.D. 65, ready-made in its Mahayanistic form, in effect of an imagine the Emperor Ming Ti (A.D. 58-- 76) of the Eastern Han dynasty in or about the year 63; though some knowledge of Buddha and his teachings existed as early as 217 B.C. As Buddha, the chief deity of Buddhism, was a guy and ended up being a god, the religion stemmed, like the others, in ancestor-worship. When a guy passes away, says this faith, his other self comes back in one form or another, "from a clod to a divinity." The way for Buddhism in China was paved by Taoism, and Buddhism reciprocally impacted Taoism by useful development of its doctrines of sanctity and immortalization. Buddhism also, as it has been well put by Dr De Groot,7 "contributed much to the ritualistic accessory of ancestor-worship. Its salvation work on behalf of the dead saved its place in Confucian China; for of Confucianism itself, piety and dedication towardss parents and forefathers, and the promotion of their joy, were the core, and, as a result, their praise with sacrifices and ceremonies was always a spiritual duty." It was hence that it was possible for the gods of Buddhism to be introduced into China and to maintain their unique characters and fulfil their unique functions without being absorbed into or submerged by the existing native religious beliefs. The result was, as we have seen, in the end a partnership instead of a relation of master and servant; and I say 'in the end' because, contrary to common belief, the Chinese have not been tolerant of foreign spiritual faiths, and at different times have maltreated Buddhism as relentlessly as they have other rivals to orthodox Confucianism.

Buddha, the Law, and the Priesthood
At the head of the Buddhist gods in China we find the triad called Buddha, the Law, and the Church, or Priesthood, which are personified as Shih-chia Fo (Shâkya), O-mi-t' o Fo (Amita), and Ju-lai Fo (Tathagata); otherwise Fo Pao, Fa Pao, and Sêng Pao (the San Pao, '3 Precious Ones')-- that is, Buddha, the prophet who came into the world to teach the Law, Dharma, the Law Immortal, and Samgha, its mystical body, Priesthood, or Church. Dharma is an entity underived, containing the spiritual aspects and product constituents of the universe. From it the other two evolve: Buddha (Shâkyamuni), the creative energy, Samgha, the totality of existence and of life. To the people these are 3 individual Buddhas, whom they worship without concerning themselves about their origin. To the priests they are just the Buddha, past, present, or future. There are also several other of these groups or triads, ten or more, composed of different divine entities, or often containing a couple of the triad already named. Shâkyamuni heads the list, having a location in at least six.

The legend of the Buddha belongs rather to Indian than to Chinese mythology and is too long to be reproduced here.

The principal gods of Buddhism are Jan-têng Fo, the Light-lamp Buddha, Mi-lo Fo (Maitrêya), the expected Messiah of the Buddhists, O-mi-t' o Fo (Amitabha or Amita), the guide who conducts his followers to the Western Paradise, Yüeh-shih Fo, the Master-physician Buddha, Ta-shih-chih P' u-sa (Mahastama), companion of Amitabha, P' i-lu Fo (Vairotchana), the greatest of the Threefold Embodiments, Kuan Yin, the Goddess of Mercy, Ti-tsang Wang, the God of Hades, Wei-t' o (Vihârapâla), the Dêva protector of the Law of Buddha and Buddhist temples, the Four Diamond Kings of Paradise, and Bodhidharma, the very first of the six Patriarchs of Eastern or Chinese Buddhism.

Diamond Kings of Heaven
On the right and left sides of the entryway hall of Buddhist temples, 2 on each side, are the massive figures of the four great Ssǔ Ta Chin-kang or T'ien- wang, the Diamond Kings of Heaven, protectors or rulers of the continents lying in the direction of the 4 cardinal points from Mount Sumêru, the centre of the world. They are 4 brothers called respectively Mo-li Ch' ing (Pure), or Tsêng Chang, Mo-li Hung (Vast), or Kuang Mu, Mo-li Hai (Sea), or To Wên, and Mo-li Shou (Age), or Ch' ih Kuo. The Chin kuang ming states that they bestow all types of happiness on those who honour the Three Treasures, Buddha, the Law, and the Priesthood. Kings and countries who disregard the Law lose their security. They are defined and represented as follows:

Mo-li Ch' ing, the oldest, is twenty-four feet in height, with a beard the hairs of which are a lot like copper wire. He carries a splendid jade ring and a spear, and always fights on foot. He has also a magic sword, 'Blue Cloud,' on the blade of which are etched the characters Ti, Shui, Huo, Fêng (Earth, Water, Fire, Wind). When brandished, it causes a black wind, which produces tens of countless spears, which pierce the bodies of guys and turn them to dust. The wind is followed by a fire, which fills the air with tens of countless golden fiery serpents. A thick smoke also rises up out of the ground, which blinds and burns guys, none being able to escape.

Mo-li Hung carries in his hand an umbrella, called the Umbrella of Chaos, formed of pearls had of spiritual properties. Opening this wonderful carry out causes the heavens and earth to be covered with thick darkness, and turning it upside down produces storms of wind and thunder and universal earthquakes.

Mo-li Hai holds a four-stringed guitar, the twanging of which transcendently impacts the earth, water, fire, or wind. When it is played all the world listens, and the camps of the enemy take fire.

Mo-li Shou has two whips and a panther-skin bag, the home of an animal resembling a white rat, known as Hua-hu Tiao. When at big this creature presumes the form of a white winged elephant, which feasts on men. He in some cases has also a snake or other man-eating creature, always prepared to obey his behests.

Legend of the Diamond Kings
The legend of the Four Diamond Kings given up the Fêng shên yen i is as follows: At the time of the combination of the Chou dynasty in the twelfth and l lth centuries B.C., Chiang Tzǔ-ya, chief counsellor to Wên Wang, and General Huang Fei-hu were safeguarding the town and mountain of Hsi-ch' i. The supporters of the house of Shang interested the four genii Mo, who lived at Chia-mêng Kuan, praying them to come to their help. They concurred, raised an army of

100,000 celestial soldiers, and traversing towns, fields, and mountains shown up in less than a day at the north gate of Hsi-ch' i, where Mo-li Ch' ing pitched his camp and entrenched his soldiers.

Hearing of this, Huang Fei-hu sped up to warn Chiang Tzǔ-ya of the danger which threatened him. "The four great generals who have just gotten to the north gate," he said, "are marvellously effective genii, professionals in all the mysteries of magic and usage of wonderful charms. It is much to be feared that we shall not have the ability to resist them."

A lot of intense fights occurred. In the beginning these entered favour of the Chin-kang, thanks to their magic weapons and particularly to Mo-li Shou's Hua-hu Tiao, who terrified the opponent by devouring their bravest warriors.

Hua-hu Tiao feasts on Yang Chien
Sadly for the Chin-kang, the brute attacked and swallowed Yang Chien, the nephew of Yü Huang. This genie, on getting in the body of the monster, lease his heart asunder and cut him in two. As he could transform himself at will, he presumed the shape of Hua-hu Tiao, and went off to Mo-li Shou, who unsuspectingly put him back into his bag.

The 4 Kings held a celebration to celebrate their accomplishment, and having drunk copiously gave themselves over to sleep. Throughout the night Yang Chien came out of the bag, with the intention of having himself of the 3 magical weapons of the Chin-kang. But he succeeded only in carrying off the umbrella of Mo-li Hung. In a subsequent engagement No-cha, the child of Vadjrâ-pani, the God of Thunder, broke the jade ring of Mo-li Ch'ing. Bad luck followed misfortune. The Chin-kang, denied of their magic weapons, began to lose heart. To complete their discomfiture, Huang T'ien Hua brought to the attack a matchless magical weapon. This was a spike 7 1/2 inches long, enclosed in a silk sheath, and called 'Heart-piercer.' It projected so strong a ray of light that eyes were blinded by it.

Huang T'ien Hua, hard pressed by Mo-li Ch'ing, drew the mysterious spike from its sheath, and hurled it at his foe. It entered his neck, and with a deep groan the giant fell dead.

Mo-li Hung and Mo-li Hai accelerated to avenge their brother, but ere they could come within striking range of Huang Ti'en Hua his redoubtable spike reached their hearts, and they lay susceptible at his feet.

The one remaining hope for the sole survivor was in Hua-hu Tiao. Mo-li Shou, not understanding that the creature had been killed, put his hand into the bag to pull him out, whereupon Yang Chien, who had returned to the bag, bit his hand off at the wrist, so that there stayed absolutely nothing but a stump of bone.

In this moment of extreme pain Mo-li Shou fell a simple prey to Huang T'ien Hua, the magic spike pierced his heart, and he fell bathed in his blood. Therefore died the last of the Chin-kang.

Chapter 12: The 3 Pure Ones

Turning to the gods of Taoism, we find that the triad or trinity, already noted as forming the head of that hierarchy, consists of three Supreme Gods, each in his own Paradise. These three Heavens, the San Ch' ing, '3 Pure Ones' (this name being also applied to the sovereigns ruling in them), were formed from the three airs, which are neighborhoods of the one prehistoric air.

The very first Paradise is Yü Ch' ing. In it reigns the very first member of the Taoist triad. He populates the Jade Mountain. The entryway to his palace is called the Golden Door. He is the source of all truth, as the sun is the source of all light.

Different authorities give his name in a different way-- Yüan-shih T'ien- tsun, or Lo Ching Hsin, and call him T'ien Pao, 'the Treasure of Heaven,' Some state that the name of the ruler of this very first Heaven is Yü Huang, and in the well-known mind he it is who occupies this supreme position. The 3 Pure Ones are above him in rank, but to him, the Pearly Emperor, is entrusted the superintendence of the world. He has all the power of Paradise and earth in his hands. He is the correlative of Heaven, or rather Heaven itself.

The second Paradise, Shang Ch' ing, is ruled by the second person of the triad, called Ling-pao T'ien- tsun, or Tao Chün. No information is given regarding his origin. He is the custodian of the spiritual books. He has existed from the beginning of the world. He computes time, dividing it into different dates. He occupies the upper pole of the world, and identifies the movements and interaction, or regulates the relations of the yin and the yang, the 2 great concepts of nature.

In the 3rd Heaven, T'ai Ch' ing, the Taoists put Lao Tzǔ, the promulgator of the real teaching drawn up by Ling-pao T'ien- tsun. He is alternatively called Shên Pao, 'the Treasure of the Spirits,' and T'ai- shang Lao-chûn, 'one of the most Distinguished Aged Ruler.' Under different presumed names he has appeared as the instructor of kings and emperors, the reformer of succeeding generations.

This three-storied Taoist Paradise, or three Paradises, is the result of the desire of the Taoists not to be out-rivalled by the Buddhists. For Buddha, the Law, and the Priesthood they substitute the Tao, or Reason, the Classics, and the Priesthood.

As regards the organization of the Taoist Heavens, Yü Huang has on his register the name of 8 hundred Taoist divinities and a plethora of Immortals. These are all split into 3 categories: Saints (Shêng-jên), Heroes (Chên-jên), and Immortals (Hsien-jên), occupying the three Paradises respectively in that order.

The Three Causes
Connected with Taoism, but not specifically associated with that faith, is the praise of the 3 Causes, the deities presiding over 3 departments of physical nature, Heaven, earth, and water.

They are known by numerous classifications: San Kuan, 'the 3 Representatives'; San Yüan, 'the 3 Origins'; San Kuan Ta Ti, 'the 3 Great Emperor Agents'; and T'ai Shang San Kuan, 'the 3 Supreme Agents.' This praise has gone through four chief phases, as follows:

The first comprises Paradise, earth, and water, T'ien, Ti, Shui, the sources of happiness, forgiveness of sins, and deliverance from evil respectively. Each of these is called King-emperor. Their names, written on labels and offered to Heaven (on a mountain), earth (by burial), and water (by immersion), are supposed to treat illness. This idea dates from the Han dynasty, being very first kept in mind about A.D. 172.

The second, San Yüan dating from A.D. 407 under the Wei dynasty, recognized the 3 Representatives with three dates of which they were respectively made the patrons. The year was split into 3 unequal parts: the very first to the seventh moon; the seventh to the tenth; and the tenth to the twelfth. Of these, the fifteenth day of the first, seventh, and tenth moons respectively became the 3 principal dates of these durations. Therefore the Representative of Heaven ended up being the primary client of the first department, honoured on the fifteenth day of the very first moon, and so on.

The 3rd phase, San Kuan, resulted from the very first two being found too complicated for popular favour. The San Kuan were the 3 sons of a man, Ch'ên Tzŭ-ch'un, who was so handsome and intelligent that the 3 daughters of Lung Wang, the Dragon-king, fell for him and went to deal with him. The oldest girl was the mom of the Superior Cause, the second of the Medium Cause, and the 3rd of the Inferior Cause. All these were gifted with superhuman powers. Yüan-shih T'ien-tsun canonized them as the 3 Great Emperor Agents of Heaven, earth, and water, governors of all beings, devils or gods, in the three regions of the universe. As in the first phase, the T'ien Kuan provides joy, the Ti Kuan grants remission of sins, and the Shui Kuan delivers from wicked or misery.

The 4th phase consisted simply in the alternative by the priests for the abstract or time-principles of the three great sovereigns of ancient times, Yao, Shun, and Yü. The literati, happy with the apotheosis of their ancient rulers, accelerated to provide incense to them, and temples, San Yüan Kung, occurred in many parts of the Empire.

A variation of the phase is the canonization, with the title of San Yüan or Three Causes, of Wu-k'o San Chên Chün, 'the 3 Real Sovereigns, Guests of the Kingdom of Wu.' They were 3 Censors who lived in the reign of King Li (Li Wang, 878-- 841 B.C.) of the Chou dynasty. Leaving the service of the Chou on account of Li's dissolute living, they went to reside in Wu, and brought success to that state in its war with the Ch'u State, then went back to their own country, and ended up being pillars of the Chou State under Li's inheritor. They appeared to secure the Emperor Chên Tsung when he was offering the Fêng-shan sacrifices on T'ai Shan in A.D. 1008, on which occasion they were canonized with the titles of Superior, Medium, and Inferior Causes, as previously, conferring upon them the regencies of Heaven, earth, and water respectively.

Yüan-shih T'ien- tsun.
Yüan-shih T'ien- tsun, or the First Cause, the Highest in Paradise, normally put at the head of the Taoist triad, is said never ever to have existed but in the fertile imagination of the Lao Tzŭist sectarians. According to them Yüan-shih T'ien- tsun had neither origin nor master, but is himself the cause of all beings, which is why he is called the First Cause.

As first member of the triad, and sovereign ruler of the First Heaven, Yü Ch' ing, where reign the saints, he is raised in rank above all the other gods. The name appointed to him is Lo Ching Hsin. He was born right before all beginnings; his substance is imperishable; it is formed basically of uncreated air, air a se, invisible and without perceptible limits. Nobody has had the ability to penetrate to the beginnings of his presence. The source of all truth, he at each remodelling of the worlds-- that is, at each new kalpa-- gives out the mystical teaching which confers immortality. All who reach this knowledge get by degrees to life everlasting, become fine-tuned like the spirits, or instantly become Immortals, even while upon earth.

Initially, Yüan-shih T'ien- tsun was not a member of the Taoist triad. He resided above the Three Paradises, above the Three Pure Ones, enduring the destructions and restorations of deep space, as a stationary rock in the midst of a stormy sea. He set the stars moving, and triggered the planets to revolve. The chief of his secret authorities was Tsao Chün, the Kitchen-god, who rendered to him an account of the good and evil deeds of each family. His executive representative was Lei Tsu, the God of Thunder, and his subordinates. The 7 stars of the North Pole were the palace of his ministers, whose offices were on the various sacred mountains. Nowadays, though, Yüan-shih T'ien- tsun is usually neglected for Yü Huang.

An Avatar of P'an Ku.
According to the custom of Chin Hung, the God of T'ai Shan of the fifth generation from P'an Ku, this being, then called Yüan-shih T'ien- wang, was an avatar of P'an Ku. It came about in this smart. In remote ages there lived on the mountains an old man, Yüan-shih T'ien- wang, who used to sit on a rock and preach to the multitude. He mentioned the greatest antiquity as if from individual experience. When Chin Hung asked him where he lived, he just raised his hand toward Heaven, iridescent clouds enveloped his body, and he responded: "Whoso wishes to know where I dwell should rise to impenetrable heights." "But how," said Chin Hung, "was he to be found in this tremendous emptiness?" Two genii, Ch' ih Ching-tzŭ and Huang Lao, then descended on the summit of T'ai Shan and said: "Let us go and visit this Yüan-shih. To do so, we need to cross the limits of the universe and pass beyond the farthest stars." Chin Hung begged them to give him their directions, to which he listened attentively. They then rose the highest of the spiritual peaks, and thence installed into the paradises, calling to him from the misty heights: "If you wish to know the origin of Yüan-shih, you need to pass beyond the confines of Paradise and earth, as he lives beyond the limitations of the worlds. You must ascend and rise till you reach the sphere of nothingness and of being, in the plains of the luminescent shadows."

Having actually reached these ethereal heights, the two genii saw a bright light, and Hsüan-hsüan Shang-jên appeared before them. The two genii acquiesced do him homage and to reveal their appreciation. "You cannot better show your appreciation," he replied, "than by making my doctrine known amongst guys. You desire," he added, "to know the history of Yüan-shih. I will tell it you. When P'an Ku had finished his work in the primitive Chaos, his spirit left its mortal envelope and found itself tossed about in empty space with no fixed assistance. 'I must,' it said, 'get born-again in noticeable form; till I can go through a brand-new birth I shall remain empty and unclear,' His soul, carried on the wings of the wind, reached Fu-yü T'ai. There it saw a saintly lady named T'ai Yüan, forty years of age, still a virgin, and living alone on Mount Ts' u-o. Air and variegated clouds were the sole nourishment of her vital spirits. A hermaphrodite, at once both the active and the passive principle, she daily scaled the greatest peak of the mountain to collect there the flowery quintessence of the sun and the moon. P'an Ku, mesmerized by her virgin pureness, benefited from a minute when she was breathing to enter her mouth in the form of a ray of light. She was enceinte for 12 years, at the end of which duration the fruit of her womb came out through her spine. From its first moment the kid could walk and speak, and its body was surrounded by a five-coloured cloud. The newly-born took the name of Yüan-shih T'ien- wang, and his mother was generally known as T'ai- yüan Shêng-mu, 'the Holy Mother of the First Cause.'".

Yü Huang.
Yü Huang means 'the Jade Emperor,' or 'the Pure August One,' jade signifying pureness. He is also known by the name Yü-huang Shang-ti, 'the Pure August Emperor on High.'.

The history of this deity, who later received a lot of honorific titles and ended up being the most popular god, a very Chinese Jupiter, appears to be rather as follows: The Emperor Ch' êng Tsung of the Sung dynasty having actually been obliged in A.D. 1005 to sign a disgraceful peace with the Tunguses or Kitans, the dynasty was in danger of losing the support of the nation. In order to hoodwink the people the Emperor constituted himself a seer, and announced with great pomp that he was in direct communication with the gods of Heaven. In doing this he was following the guidance of his crafty and unreliable minister Wang Ch' in-jo, who had often tried to persuade him that the pretended revelations credited to Fu Hsi, Yü Wang, and others were only pure innovations to induce obedience. The Emperor, having studied his part well, assembled his ministers in the tenth moon of the year 1012, and made to them the following statement: "In a dream I had a go to from an Immortal, who brought me a letter from Yü Huang, the profess of which was as follows: 'I have already sent you by your forefather Chao [T'ai Tsu] two celestial missives. Now I am going to send him personally to visit you.'" A bit after his forefather T'ai Tsu, the founder of the dynasty, came according to Yü Huang's guarantee, and Ch' êng Tsung quickened to inform his ministers of it. This is the beginning of Yü Huang. He was born of a scams, and came ready-made from the brain of an emperor.

The Cask of Pearls.
Fearing to be advised for the fraud by another of his ministers, the academic Wang Tan, the Emperor fixed to put a golden gag in his mouth. So one day, having actually welcomed him to a banquet, he overwhelmed him with flattery and made him intoxicated with great white wine. "I

would like the members of your family also to taste this wine," he added, "so I am making you a present of a cask of it." When Wang Tan returned home, he found the cask filled with precious pearls. Out of thankfulness to the Emperor he kept quiet as to the fraud, and made no more opposition to his plans, but when on his death-bed he asked that his head be shaved like a priest's and that he be clothed in priestly robes so that he may expiate his criminal offense of feebleness right before the Emperor.

K'ang Hsi, the great Emperor of the Ch' ing dynasty, who had already declared that if it is really wrong to assign deceit to a man it is still more reprehensible to assign a fraud to Heaven, stigmatized him as follows: "Wang Tan committed two faults: the very first was in demonstrating himself a repellent flatterer of his Prince throughout his life; the second was in ending up being a worshipper of Buddha at his death."

The Legend of Yü Huang

So much for historic record. The legend of Yü Huang relates that in old times there existed a kingdom called Kuang Yen Miao Lo Kuo, whose king was Ching Tê, his queen being called Pao Yüeh. Though getting on in years, the latter had no child. The Taoist priests were summoned by edict to the palace to perform their rites. They recited prayers with the thing of obtaining a successor to the throne. Throughout the occurring night the Queen had a vision. Lao Chün appeared to her, riding a dragon, and carrying a male child in his arms. He drifted down through the air in her direction. The Queen pled him to give her the child as a successor to the throne. "I am rather willing," he said. "Here it is." She fell on her knees and thanked him. On waking she found herself enceinte. At the end of a year the Prince was born. From an early age he revealed to himself thoughtful and generous to the poor. On the death of his father he rose the throne, but after ruling just a couple of days abandoned in favour of his chief minister, and ended up being a hermit at P' u-ming, in Shensi, and also on Mount Hsiu Yen, in Yünnan. Having actually attained to excellence, he passed the rest of his days in curing illness and saving life; and it was in the workout of these charitable deeds that he passed away. The emperors Ch' êng Tsung and Hui Tsung, of the Sung dynasty, loaded him with all the different titles associated with his name at the present day.

Both Buddhists and Taoists claim him as their own, the former determining him with Indra, in which case Yü Huang is a Buddhist deity integrated into the Taoist temple. He has also been required the subject of a 'nature myth.' The Emperor Ching Tê, his father, is the sun, the Queen Pao Yüeh the moon, and the marriage symbolizes the rebirth of the vivifying power which outfits nature with green plants and gorgeous flowers.

T'ung- t' ien Chiao-chu

In modern Taoism T'ung- t' ien Chiao-chu is considered the very first of the Patriarchs and one of the most powerful genii of the sect. His master was Hung-chün Lao-tsu. He wore a red bathrobe embroidered with white cranes, and rode a k' uei niu, a beast resembling a buffalo, with one long horn like a unicorn. His palace, the Pi Yu Kung, was situated on Mount Tzǔ Chih Yai.

This genie took the part of Chou Wang and helped him to resist Wu Wang's armies. First, he sent his disciple To-pao Tao-jên to Chieh-p' ai Kuan. He gave him four valuable swords and the plan of a fort which he was to construct and to call Chu-hsien Chên, 'the Citadel of all the Immortals.'

To-pao Tao-jên performed his orders, but he had to combat a fight with Kuang Ch' êng-tzŭ, and the latter, equipped with a celestial seal, struck his enemy so hard that he fell to the ground and needed to take refuge in flight.

T'ung- t' ien Chiao-chu came to the defence of his disciple and to restore the spirits of his forces. Unfortunately, a posse of gods came to assist Wu Wang's powerful general, Chiang Tzŭ-ya. The very first who attacked T'ung- t' ien Chiao-chu was Lao Tzŭ, who struck him some times with his stick. Then came Chun T' i, armed with his walking stick. The buffalo of T'ung- t' ien Chiao-chu stamped him under foot, and Chun T' i was tossed to the earth, and only just had time to rise up quickly and mount into the air amid a great cloud of dust.

There could be no doubt that the battle was going against T'ung- t' ien Chiao-chu; to finish his discomfiture Jan-têng Tao-jên cleft the air and fell upon him unexpectedly. With a violent blow of his 'Fix-sea' staff he cast him down and obliged him to forfeit the struggle.

T'ung- t' ien Chiao-chu then prepared prepare for a new fortified camp beyond T'ung Kuan, and tried to take the offensive again, but again Lao Tzŭ stopped him with a blow of his stick. Yüan-shih T'ien- tsun wounded his shoulder with his jewel Ju-i, and Chun-t' i Tao-jên waved his 'Branch of the Seven Virtues.' Immediately the magic sword of T'ung- t' ien Chiao-chu was minimized to splinters, and he saved himself only by flight.

Hung-chün Lao-tsu, the master of these 3 genii, seeing his three cherished disciples in the mêlée, fixed to make peace between them. He put together all 3 in a camping tent in Chiang Tzŭ-ya's camp, made them kneel right before him, then reproached T'ung- t' ien Chiao-chu at length for having taken the part of the tyrant Chou, and suggested them in future to reside in consistency. After finishing his speech, he produced three tablets, and ordered each of the genii to swallow one. When they had done so, Hung-chün Lao-tsu said to them: "I have given you these pills to ensure an inviolable truce among you. Know that the very first who captivates an idea of discord in his heart will find that the tablet will explode in his stomach and trigger his immediate death."

Hung-chün Lao-tsu then took T'ung- t' ien Chiao-chu away with him on his cloud to Heaven.

Immortals, Heroes, Saints
A Never-ceasing, according to Taoist tradition, is a solitary man of the mountains. He appears to die, but does not. After 'death' his body keeps all the qualities of the living. The body or dead body is for him only a way of shift, a stage of transformation-- a cocoon or chrysalis, the short-term home of the butterfly.

To reach this state a hygienic regimen both of the body and mind need to be observed. All luxury, greed, and ambition must be avoided. But negation is inadequate. In the system of nutrition all the aspects which enhance the essence of the constituent yin and yang principles need to be found by methods of medicine, chemistry, gymnastic exercises, etc. When the maximum essential force has been gotten the means of maintaining it and keeping it from the attacks of death and disease should be found; in a word, he must spiritualize himself-- render himself totally independent of matter. All the experiments have for their item the saving in the tablets of immortality the aspects essential for the development of the vital force and for the constitution of a new spiritual and super-humanized being. In this rising perfection there are some grades:

(1) The Immortal (Hsien). The very first stage consists in bringing about the birth of the superhuman in the ascetic's person, which reaching excellence leaves the earthly body, like the grasshopper its sheath. This first stage attained, the Never-ceasing journeys at will throughout the universe, enjoys all the advantages of perfect health without fearing disease or death, consumes copiously-- absolutely nothing is wanting to complete his joy.

(2) The Perfect Man, or Hero (Chên-jên). The 2nd stage is a greater one. The entire body is spiritualized. It has ended up being so subtle, so spiritual, that it can fly in the air. Born upon the wings of the wind, seated on the clouds of Paradise, it takes a trip from one world to another and fixes its habitation in the stars. It is freed from all laws of matter, but is, however, not entirely changed into pure spirit.

(3) The Saint (Shêng-jên). The third stage is that of the superhuman entities or saints. They are those who have achieved to amazing intelligence and virtue.

The God of the Immortals
Mu Kung or Tung Wang Kung, the God of the Immortals, was also called I Chün Ming and Yü Huang Chün, the Prince Yü Huang.

The primitive vapour hardened, remained inactive for a time, and after that produced living entities, beginning with the development of Mu Kung, the purest compound of the Eastern Air, and sovereign of the active male principle yang and of all the nations of the East. His palace is in the misty heavens, violet clouds form its dome, blue clouds its walls. Hsien T'ung, 'the Immortal Youth,' and Yü Nü, 'the Jade Maiden,' are his servants. He keeps the register of all the Immortals, male and woman.

Hsi Wang Mu
Hsi Wang Mu was created out of the pure quintessence of the Western Air, in the legendary continent of Shên Chou. She is typically called the Golden Mom of the Tortoise.

Her family name is otherwise given as Hou, Yang, and Ho. Her own name was Hui, and given name Wan-chin. She had 9 sons and twenty-four daughters.

As Mu Kung, formed of the Eastern Air, is the active principle of the male air and sovereign of the Eastern Air, so Hsi Wang Mu, born of the Western Air, is the passive or female principle (yin) and sovereign of the Western Air. These 2 concepts, co-operating, engender Paradise and earth and all the beings of deep space, and hence become the two principles of life and of the subsistence of all that exists. She is the head of the troop of genii house on the K'un- lun Mountains (the Taoist equivalent of the Buddhist Sumêru), and from time to time holds sexual intercourse with favoured royal votaries.

The Banquet of Peaches
Hsi Wang Mu's palace is positioned in the high mountains of the snowy K'un- lun. It is 1000 li (about 333 miles) in circuit; a rampart of massive gold surrounds its battlements of precious stones. Its right wing rises up on the edge of the Kingfishers' River. It is the normal home of the Immortals, who are divided into seven unique categories according to the colour of their garments-- red, blue, black, violet, yellow, green, and 'nature-colour.' There is a marvellous fountain built of jewels, where the periodical banquet of the Immortals is held. This feast is called P'an- t' ao Hui, 'the Banquet of Peaches.' It occurs on the borders of the Yao Ch' ih, Lake of Gems, and is attended by both male and female Immortals. Besides some superfine meats, they are served with bears' paws, monkeys' lips, dragons' liver, phoenix marrow, and peaches gathered in the orchard, endowed with the mystic virtue of conferring longevity on all who have the all the best to taste them. It was by these peaches that the date of the banquet was repaired. The tree put forth leaves once every 3 thousand years, and it needed three 1,000 years after that for the fruit to ripen. These were Hsi Wang Mu's birthdays, when all the Immortals assembled for the great banquet, "the occasion being more joyful than solemn, for there was music on invisible instruments, and songs not from mortal tongues."

Chapter 13: The First Taoist Pope

Chang Tao-ling, the very first Taoist pope, was born in A.D. 35, in the reign of the Emperor Kuang Wu Ti of the Han dynasty. His birth place is variously given as the T'ien- mu Shan, 'Eye of Paradise Mountain,' in Lin-an Hsien, in Chekiang, and Fêng-yang Fu, in Anhui. He committed himself wholly to study and meditation, decreasing all deals to enter the service of the State. He preferred to use up his home in the mountains of Western China, where he persevered in the research study of alchemy and in cultivating the virtues of pureness and mental abstraction. From the hands of Lao Tzŭ he received superly a mystic writing, by following the instructions in which he was successful in his search for the elixir of life.

One day when he was participated in experimenting with the 'Dragon-tiger elixir' a soul appeared to him and said: "On Po-sung Mountain is a stone house in which are hidden the works of the 3 Emperors of antiquity and a canonical work. By getting these you might rise to Heaven, if you go through the course of discipline they prescribe."

Chang Tao-ling found these works, and by methods of them got the power of flying, of hearing far-off noises, and of leaving his body. After going through a 1000 days of discipline, and receiving instruction from a goddess, who taught him to perambulate amongst the stars, he proceeded to eliminate with the king of the devils, to divide mountains and seas, and to command the wind and thunder. All the devils fled right before him. On account of the prodigious massacre of demons by this hero the wind and thunder were decreased to subjection, and different divinities came with eager haste to acknowledge their faults. In nine years he got the power to rise to Heaven.

The Founder of Modern Taoism
Chang Tao-ling might appropriately be thought about as the true founder of contemporary Taoism. The dishes for the tablets of immortality contained in the strange books, and the creation of talismans for the cure of all sorts of maladies, not only exalted him to the high position he has since occupied in the minds of his numerous disciples, but allowed them in turn to exploit effectively this brand-new source of power and wealth. From that time the Taoist sect began to concentrate on the art of healing. Protecting or treating talismans bearing the Master's seal were purchased for huge sums. It is thus seen that he was after all a deceiver of the people, and unbelievers or competing partisans of other sects have called him a 'rice-thief'-- which perhaps he was.

He is typically represented as clothed in highly embellished garments, displaying with his right hand his magic sword, keeping in his left a cup including the draught of immortality, and riding a tiger which in one paw understands his magic seal and with the others squashes down the five venomous beings: lizard, snake, spider, toad, and centipede. Pictures of him with these accessories are pasted up in houses on the 5th day of the fifth moon to forfend disaster and sickness.

The Peach-gathering

It is related of him that, not wanting to ascend to Paradise too soon, he took part of only half of the pill of immortality, dividing the other half amongst several of his admirers, and that he had at least two selves or personalities, one of which used to disport itself in a boat on a small lake in front of his home. The other self would receive his visitors, entertaining them with food and drink and instructional discussion. On one occasion this self said to them: "You are unable to quit the world altogether as I can, but by mimicing my example in the matter of family relations you could acquire a medication which would lengthen your lives by some centuries. I have given the crucible in which Huang Ti prepared the draught of immortality to my disciple Wang Ch' ang. Later on, a man will come from the East, who also will use it. He will arrive on the seventh day of the first moon."

Exactly on that day there arrived from the East a man called Chao Shêng, who was the person indicated by Chang Tao-ling. He was acknowledged by a symptom of himself he had caused to appear in advance of his coming. Chang then led all his disciples, to the number of three hundred, to the greatest peak of the Yün-t'ai. Below them they saw a peach-tree growing near a pointed rock, extending its branches like arms above a fathomless abyss. It was a large tree, covered with ripe fruit. Chang said to his disciples: "I will communicate a spiritual formula to the one among you who will dare to collect the fruit of that tree." They all leaned over to look, but each declared the task to be impossible. Chao Shêng alone had the nerve to hurry out to the point of the rock and up the tree stretching out into space. With firm foot he stood and gathered the peaches, putting them in the folds of his cloak, as many as it would hold, but when he wished to climb back up the precipitous slope, his hands slipped on the smooth rock, and all his attempts failed. Appropriately, he threw the peaches, three hundred and 2 in all, one by one up to Chang Tao-ling, who distributed them. Each disciple ate one, as also did Chang, who reserved the remaining one for Chao Shêng, whom he helped to climb again. To do this Chang extended his arm to a length of thirty feet, all present marvelling at the miracle. After Chao had eaten his peach Chang was standing on the edge of the precipice, and said with a laugh: "Chao Shêng was brave enough to climb out to that tree and his foot never tripped. I too will make the effort. If I prosper I will have a big peach as a benefit." Having actually spoken thus, he jumped into space, and alighted in the branches of the peach-tree. Wang Ch'ang and Chao Shêng also jumped into the tree and stood one on each side of him. There Chang communicated to them the strange formula. 3 days later they went back to their homes; then, having made final arrangements, they repaired once again to the mountain peak, whence, in the presence of the other disciples, who followed them with their eyes until they had entirely vanished from view, all three rose to Heaven in the daylight.

Chang Tao-ling's Great Power

The name of Chang Tao-ling, the Heavenly Teacher, is a household word in China. He is on the earth the Vicegerent of the Pearly Emperor in Heaven, and the Commander-in-Chief of the pure hosts of Taoism. He, the leader of the wizards, the 'real [i.e. ideal] man,' as he is called, wields an enormous spiritual power throughout the land. The present pope boasts of an unbroken line for three-score generations. His family obtained possession of the Dragon-tiger Mountain in Kiangsi about A.D. 1000. "This personage," says a pre-Republican writer, "assumes a state which mimics the imperial. He confers buttons like an emperor. Priests pertain to him from numerous cities and temples to get big promotion, whom he invests with titles and presents with seals of office."

Kings of Paradise
The 4 Kings of Heaven, Ssŭ Ta T'ien- wang, reside on Mount Sumêru (Hsü-mi Shan), the centre of deep space. It is 3,360,000 li-- that is, about a million miles-- high.9 Its eastern slope is of gold, its western of silver, its south-eastern of crystal, and its north-eastern of agate. The Four Kings seem the Taoist reflection of the 4 Chin-kang of Buddhism already noticed. Their names are Li, Ma, Chao, and Wên. They are represented as holding a pagoda, sword, 2 swords, and spiked club respectively. Their praise appears to be due to their advantageous appearance and aid on various critical occasions in the dynastic history of the T'ang and Sung Periods.

T'ai I.
Forehead are found in different parts committed to T'ai I, the Great One, or Great Unity. When Emperor Wu Ti (140-- 86 B.C.) of the Han dynasty was in search of the secret of immortality, and various ideas had proved unacceptable, a Taoist priest, Miao Chi, told the Emperor that his really want of success was because of his omission to sacrifice to T'ai I, the first of the celestial spirits, pricing quote the classical precedent of antiquity found in the Book of History. The Emperor, believing his word, ordered the Grand Master of Sacrifices to re-establish this worship at the capital. He followed thoroughly the prescriptions of Miao Chi. This enraged the literati, who fixed to ruin him. One day, when the Emperor was about to drink among his potions, among the chief courtiers seized the cup and drank the contents himself. The Emperor was about to have him killed, when he said: "Your Majesty's order is unnecessary; if the potion gives immortality, I cannot be killed; if, on the other hand, it does not, your Majesty must reimburse me for negating the pretensions of the Taoist priest." The Emperor, however, was not convinced.

One account represents T'ai I as having resided in the time of Shên Nung, the Divine Husbandman, who visited him to speak with him on the subjects of diseases and fortune. He was Hsien Yüan's medical preceptor. His medical knowledge was given to future generations. He was one of those who, with the Immortals, was welcomed to the great Peach Assembly of the Western Royal Mom.

As the spirit of the star T'ai I he resides in the Eastern Palace, listening for the sobs of patients so as to save them. For this purpose he presumes numberless forms in various regions. With a boat of lotus-flowers of nine colours he ferries guys over to the shore of salvation. Keeping in his hand a willow-branch, he scatters from it the dew of the doctrine.

T'ai I is otherwise represented as the Ruler of the Five Celestial Sovereigns, Cosmic Matter before it caked into concrete shapes, the Triune Spirit of Heaven, earth, and T'ai I as 3 different beings, an unknown Spirit, the Spirit of the Pole Star, etc., but virtually the Taoists confine their T'ai I to T'ai- i Chên-jên, in which Perfect Man they personify the abstract philosophical concepts.10.

Goddess of the North Star.

Tou Mu, the Bushel Mother, or Goddess of the North Star, worshipped by both Buddhists and Taoists, is the Indian Maritchi, and was made an excellent divinity by the Taoists. She is said to have been the mother of the nine Jên Huang or Human Sovereigns of wonderful antiquity, who succeeded the lines of Celestial and Terrestrial Sovereigns. She occupies in the Taoist religion the exact same relative position as Kuan Yin, who may be said to be the heart of Buddhism. Having attained to a profound knowledge of celestial mysteries, she shone with divine light, could cross the seas, and pass from the sun to the moon. She also had a kind heart for the sufferings of humanity. The King of Chou Yü, in the north, married her on hearing of her tons of virtues. They had nine sons. Yüan-shih T'ien- tsun came to earth to welcome her, her husband, and 9 sons to enjoy the thrills of Heaven. He placed her in the palace Tou Shu, the Pivot of the Pole, since all the other stars revolve round it, and gave her the title of Queen of the Teaching of Primitive Heaven. Her 9 sons have their palaces in the neighbouring stars.

Tou Mu wears the Buddhist crown, is seated on a lotus throne, has three eyes, eighteen arms, and holds numerous precious things in her many hands, like a bow, spear, sword, flag, dragon's head, pagoda, five chariots, sun's disk, moon's disk, and so on. She has control of the books of life and death, and all who wish to prolong their days praise at her shrine. Her devotees abstain from animal food on the 3rd and twenty-seventh day of every month.

Of her sons, two are the Northern and Southern Bushels; the latter, dressed in red, guidelines birth; the former, in white, guidelines death. "A young Esau once found them on the South Mountain, under a tree, playing chess, and by a deal of venison his lease of life was extended from nineteen to ninety-nine years."

Snorter and Blower

At the time of the defeat of the Shang and facility of the Chou dynasty in 1122 B.C. there lived two marshals, Chêng Lung and Ch' ên Ch' i. These were Hêng and Ha, the Snorter and Blower respectively.

The previous was the primary superintendent of supplies for the armies of the autocrat emperor Chou, the Nero of China. The latter supervised of the victualling department of the exact same army.

From his master, Tu O, the popular Taoist magician of the K'un- lun Mountains, Hêng acquired a wonderful power. When he snorted, his nostrils, with a sound like that of a bell, produced two white columns of light, which damaged his enemies, body and soul. Hence through him the Chou gained many victories. But one day he was caught, bound, and taken to the general of Chou. His life was spared, and he was made general superintendent of army stores as well as generalissimo of 5 army corps. Later he found himself deal with to face with the Blower. The latter had learnt from the magician how to store in his chest a supply of yellow gas which, when he blew it out, annihilated anybody whom it struck. By this means he triggered large spaces to be made in the ranks of the enemy.

Being opposed to one another, the one snorting out great streaks of white light, the other blowing streams of yellow gas, the combat continued till the Blower was injured in the shoulder by No-cha, of the army of Chou, and pierced in the stomach with a spear by Huang Fei-hu, Yellow Flying Tiger

The Snorter in turn was slain in this battle by Marshal Chin Ta-shêng, 'Golden Big Pint,' who was an ox-spirit and endowed with the mystical power of producing in his entrails the renowned niu huang, ox-yellow, or bezoar. Dealing with the Snorter, he spat in his face, with a noise like thunder, a piece of bezoar as large as a rice-bowl. It struck him on the nose and split his nostrils. He fell down to the earth, and was instantly cut in 2 by a blow from his victor's sword.

After the Chou dynasty had been definitely established Chiang Tzŭ-ya canonized the 2 marshals Hêng and Ha, and conferred on them the offices of guardians of the Buddhist temple gates, where their enormous images may be seen.

Blue Dragon and White Tiger.
The functions discharged by Hêng and Ha at the gateways of Buddhist temples are in Taoist temples released by Blue Dragon and White Tiger.

The former, the Spirit of the Blue Dragon Star, was Têng Chiu-kung, one of the chief generals of the last emperor of the Yin dynasty. He had a boy named Têng Hsiu, and a daughter called Ch'an-yü.

The army of Têng Chiu-kung was camped at San-shan Kuan, when he got orders to proceed to the battle then taking place at Hsi Ch'i. There, in withstanding No-cha and Huang Fei-hu, he had his left arm broken by the former's magic bracelet, but, thankfully for him, his subordinate, T'u Hsing-sun, a distinguished magician, gave him a solution which quickly healed the fracture.

His daughter then emerged to avenge her father. She had a magic weapon, the Five-fire Stone, which she tossed full in the face of Yang Chien. But the Immortal was not wounded; on the other hand, his celestial pet dog leapt at Ch'an-yü and bit her neck, so that she was obliged to leave. T'u Hsing-sun, however, recovered the injury.

After a banquet, Têng Chiu-kung promised his daughter in a marriage relationship to T'u Hsing-sun if he would get him the triumph at Hsi Ch'i. Chiang Tzŭ-ya then persuaded T'u's magic master, Chü Liu-sun, to call his disciple over to his camp, where he asked him why he was battling against the brand-new dynasty. "Since," he replied, "Chiu-kung has promised me his daughter in marriage as a benefit of success." Chiang Tzŭ-ya thereupon promised to acquire the bride, and sent a force to take her. As a result of the battling that occurred, Chiu-kung was beaten, and pulled away in confusion, leaving Ch'an-yü in the hands of the victors. Throughout the next couple of days, the marriage was celebrated with great event in the victor's camp. According to custom-made, the bride-to-be returned for some days to her father's home, and while there she earnestly exhorted Chiu-kung to submit. Following her advice, he visited Chiang Tzŭ-ya's party.

In the ensuing battles he combated valiantly on the side of his former enemy, and killed tons of famous warriors, but he was eventually attacked by the Blower, from whose mouth a column of yellow gas struck him, tossing him from his steed. He was made prisoner, and performed by order of General Ch'iu Yin. Chiang Tzŭ-ya provided on him the kingdom of heaven Dragon Star.

The Spirit of the White Tiger Star is Yin Ch'êng-hsiu. His dad, Yin P'o-pai, a high courtier of the tyrant Chou Wang, was sent out to negotiate peace with Chiang Tzŭ-ya but was taken and put to death by Marquis Chiang Wên-huan. His son, attempting to avenge his dad's murder, was pierced by a spear, and his head was cut off and carried in accomplishment to Chiang Tzŭ-ya.

As compensation he was, though rather tardily, canonized as the Spirit of the White Tiger Star.

Made in the USA
Las Vegas, NV
19 September 2021